# THE CASE IS CLOSED... ALMOST

"But look at it like this, love," Antony said. "There's no way on Earth of proving they were murdered."

"I suppose not," Jenny said doubtfully. She heaved a small sigh that might have been one of relief and for the first time picked up her glass. "I'm sure Vera will agree there's nothing more to be done."

"I dare say she will." Antony too began to sip his sherry and smiled at her.

It was perhaps as well for their peace of mind that neither of them had any idea at that moment how drastically things were to be changed by morning...

# THEY STAY FOR DEATH

## Sara Woods

They have said their prayers, and they stay for death.
*King Henry V*, Act IV, scene ii

AVON BOOKS NEW YORK

Any work of fiction whose characters were of uniform excellence would rightly be condemned—by that fact if by no other—as being incredibly dull. Therefore no excuse can be considered necessary for the villainy or folly of the people appearing in this book. It seems extremely unlikely that any one of them should resemble a real person, alive or dead. Any such resemblance is completely unintentional and without malice.

S.W.

AVON BOOKS
A division of
The Hearst Corporation
105 Madison Avenue
New York, New York 10016

Copyright © 1980 by Sara Woods
Front cover illustration by Dave Calver
Published by arrangement with the St. Martin's Press
Library of Congress Catalog Card Number: 79-27321
ISBN 0-380-70587-7

First Avon Books Printing: December 1988

AVON TRADEMARK REG. U.S. PAT. OFF. AND IN OTHER COUNTRIES, MARCA REGISTRADA, HECHO EN U.S.A.

Printed in the U.S.A.

K-R 10 9 8 7 6 5 4 3 2 1

# PART I

# THE CHRISTMAS RECESS, 1972

# TUESDAY, 4th January

## I

'Got something to ask you,' said Vera, Lady Harding. She had her own abrupt, elliptical way of speaking, but none of her audience, who comprised her immediate family, thought the worse of her for that.

'Well, you know, Vera,' said Antony Maitland obligingly, 'if there's anything at all I can do for you – ' It wasn't until later that he realised that, besides being obliging, he had also been extremely unwary.

'I hope you know what you're letting yourself in for,' said Sir Nicholas Harding, indulgently. It was undeniable that, in the months since his marriage, he had mellowed considerably, but his nephew for one wasn't on that account going to trust his apparent amiability an inch. Another thing Antony wasn't at all sure about was whether this sudden request of Vera's was as much of a surprise to his uncle as it was to himself.

A moment later he got his answer. 'The name Chedcombe has been mentioned,' said Sir Nicholas, with undeniably provocative intent.

'I hate the place,' said Antony uncompromisingly. His wife, Jenny, began to lose some of her serene look, and cast an anxious glance in Vera's direction. But Vera was concentrated on her problem, and did not notice.

'Mainly on my account, wasn't it?' she said. Her gruff tones could hardly be called persuasive, but that was obviously her intention. 'If you think about it – '

'Why should I?' Antony asked her.

'It isn't,' said Vera, who had her own way of dealing with recalcitrance, 'as if there were a definite problem I could propound to you. Just a lot of gossip.' On her marriage to

Sir Nicholas some five months before, she had acquired the status of his aunt-by-marriage, but both of them found it difficult to remember that.

'That figures,' said Antony, and saw his uncle close his eyes as if in pain. 'I mean, you know, that's one thing you can count on in Chedcombe. Gossip.'

'I know you've said often enough you never wanted to go back there,' said Vera hastily. 'But this is something . . . rather a nasty business. If only you'd listen, Antony.'

'I said, didn't I, anything I could do?' Maitland sounded rueful now. But then he added more cheerfully, 'A promise tricked out of one isn't really a promise at all . . . don't you think?'

'Decide when you've heard what I've got to say,' said Vera doggedly. Jenny took a quick look round; but, seeing that both her husband and their guests were supplied with coffee and cognac, there was nothing for it but to sit back, fold her hands, and prepare to listen.

Maitland, whose instinct was always towards movement when anything disturbed him, got up and kicked the fire into something more resembling a blaze. He remained standing on the hearthrug, looking down at Vera, and there was something a little sombre in his expression now. 'Tell me,' he said, but without any of the expansiveness with which he had originally greeted her request.

'Friend of mine,' said Vera. 'Mary Dudley. She's worried.'

'Is that all there is of the story?' asked Antony, after a moment. 'Because if so —'

Vera gave him a rather helpless look. When she had been at the Bar herself on the West Midland circuit she had managed to find words enough to protect her clients' interests. But now any claims to eloquence seemed to have deserted her. Sir Nicholas said smoothly into the silence that developed, 'We'd better explain to you, Antony, that Miss Dudley is the matron of the Restawhile Hotel.'

'Oh, God!' said Antony, who didn't often indulge in blasphemy. And then, 'What the devil does a hotel want with a Matron?' he asked reasonably.

8

'It's really an old people's home.'

'Then why doesn't it come out into the open and say so?'

'A very expensive, exclusive place,' explained Sir Nicholas, who seemed to take some obscure delight in the story he was telling. 'There's a nursing-home attached; you'd better explain about the nursing-home, Vera.'

'They do have a few chronic patients,' said Vera. 'But mostly it's just there to take care of the other residents when they're taken sick. That happens quite often, as you can imagine.'

'Is this – this friend of yours a qualified nurse?'

'Good Heavens, yes, and so are her staff. There is also a doctor in regular attendance. The patients really get the best of care.'

'And the hotel side?'

'That's staffed separately, and very well too, so Mary always said. I think you can take it she's right about that, she's always been something of a perfectionist.'

'Well, that's all very fine. What's the trouble?'

Again Vera hesitated, and looked at her husband as though asking his assistance. That, thought Antony, was something new, if she was giving up a little of her independence of thought. Vera was tall for a woman, and rather heavily built, but more elegant now than she had been in the days when he first knew her. She still favoured sack-like garments, but somehow they had acquired an air of being well-cut, and as an added bonus she was learning what colours suited her. But there was never, he thought – and was pleased by the thought – going to be very much change in the essential Vera, whose thick greying hair was always escaping, like the White Queen's, from its confining pins.

Sir Nicholas was ready enough to rise to the occasion. 'The trouble is . . . death!' he said, with a touch of drama that neither Antony nor Jenny ever remembered hearing in his voice before. 'Three deaths, to be exact.'

'Among the chronic patients?'

'No, that's the trouble. Guests in the hotel, who happened to be taken ill and moved into the nursing-home wing.'

9

'How many deaths did you say?'

'Three, within a space of six months. That's really all you need to know about it, my dear boy, because you can understand in a place like Chedcombe –'

'I understand that all right.' Maitland's tone was as grim as Vera's had been a few minutes before. 'But there are other things I should like to know, if you don't mind. For instance, exactly how old were these three old people?'

Vera was ready with the answer to that. 'The first one was eighty-nine,' she said. 'The second only seventy-six, and the third, I think, just over eighty.'

'Then was it really so surprising – ?'

'That's precisely what I said,' put in Sir Nicholas in a pleased tone.

'The doctor didn't think so. He had attended all of them from time to time, and made no bones about signing the death certificates. But after the second death the talk started, and Mary says it has now reached a pitch where she's almost afraid to go out. The shops –'

'Yes, I remember,' said Antony, smiling at her affectionately. 'The first time we worked together the shops – as well as everyone else in Chedcombe, as far as I could make out – resented your bringing in an outsider, and you had difficulty in getting served. But surely a place like this – this hotel – ?'

'It's Mary's personal shopping she finds difficult,' said Vera, 'and some of the nurses are having the same trouble. But that isn't the worst of it really, it's the atmosphere . . . you know what Chedcombe is like, Antony!'

'Yes, I know only too well. The question is,' he added, looking from Vera to Sir Nicholas, and then glancing at Jenny, on whose sympathy he thought he could rely, 'What am I expected to do about it?'

'The Hilary Term doesn't start for a few days yet,' said Vera, very much in earnest, 'and Nicholas tells me the first case you have coming up has been postponed.'

'My client's in hospital,' Maitland agreed. 'But there are other things that I could be working on, you know.'

'But nothing absolutely urgent. A few days – ' said Vera enticingly. 'You agree with me, don't you, Jenny?'

'I might,' said Jenny cautiously. 'But, honestly, Vera, I don't see what Antony can do about it. Is it the suggestion that all these people have been murdered?'

'That's what the town is saying.'

'Do you believe it?'

'At least I'm sure that Mary – '

Antony rushed in to stop her there. He sometimes thought that the phrase 'they wouldn't do a thing like that' was the bane of his life. To hear it from Vera, who as a barrister herself ought to have known better, took him aback a little. 'You're asking me to prove that the deaths were natural,' he said. 'I don't think that comes quite within my province, do you?'

'Asking you to find out the truth,' Vera corrected him. 'I've no means of knowing whether that's the same thing.'

Sir Nicholas evidently thought it was time he took a hand again. He and his nephew were both tall, but the older man was far more heavily built, and much more conventionally good-looking; sufficiently so, in fact, to invite the description 'handsome' in the newspapers, to the detriment of his temper. He had fair hair – so fair that it was impossible to tell whether there was any grey in it – and an unconsciously authoritative manner. Just now, he was concerned about his wife's peace of mind. 'The Assize – the Crown Court – won't be sitting yet,' he pointed out. 'There's no reason why you shouldn't take Jenny with you, have a few days' holiday.'

'At this time of year?'

'I've known you spend time in the wilds of Yorkshire in considerably worse weather than this,' said his uncle unsympathetically. 'The hotel – what's its name? – the George, is warm and comfortable, I don't see why you shouldn't enjoy the change.'

'But it won't *be* a change,' Antony protested. 'If you think I enjoy asking questions – '

'In a good cause,' said Sir Nicholas solemnly. 'You may not care about Miss Dudley's peace of mind, but Vera does.'

'Chedcombe doesn't like me any more than I like it. I'd have to go in an absolutely private capacity, anything else would only make matters worse. And even so —'

'Should like to feel we'd done what we could,' said Vera, becoming gruffer than ever as she sensed victory in the offing. 'You see,' she added in a rush, 'I don't altogether trust that doctor.'

'Have you any reason for saying that, or is it just feminine intuition?'

'Nothing of the sort!' Vera was a little ruffled by the suggestion. Then she gave one of her short barks of laughter. 'Not that I can explain the reason exactly,' she admitted. 'But you can see why I think . . . sort of thing you'd do well, Antony, but not my kind of thing at all.'

Antony came back to his chair and picked up his cognac. His coffee had grown cold now and would probably still be there when they came to clear away later. 'How do you feel about a day or two in the country, love?' he asked Jenny, smiling at her.

She knew as well as he did that this was capitulation, a thing she had been in no doubt about from the beginning. 'I don't think it will be much fun for you, but I shall enjoy it well enough,' she said.

'Then the sooner the better.' He had been sipping his brandy, and perhaps that had put heart into him. 'When can you be ready?'

'Any time you say.'

'All right then, we'll go tomorrow,' he told her; and he did not know, as he spoke, how much he was later to regret the words.

Sir Nicholas exchanged a look with his wife, and then turned to his nephew. 'If you could contrive to be a little less sudden in your decisions, Antony,' he said.

'That's what you wanted, isn't it?' The humour of the situation struck him suddenly and he began to laugh. 'I hadn't a hope from the beginning,' he said, 'with you and Vera ganging up on me. But I hope you realise that there are quite a lot of questions I want answering before we go.'

The Maitlands occupied, as they had done for many years now, the two top floors of Sir Nicholas Harding's house, number 5 Kempenfeldt Square. Funnily enough, the whole of the north side on which number 5 was situated remained in private hands, though the houses on the other three sides had now almost entirely been converted to some commercial use. In the beginning the division had been intended as a purely temporary arrangement, during a period of acute housing shortage, and the conversion had not been done so drastically as to make the two parts of the house self-contained. Over the years they had all forgotten the word 'temporary', it might have been wiped from their vocabulary; the arrangement was convenient, and at most times pleasant, and even when it wasn't – that is, on the occasions when Sir Nicholas's unpredictable temper was causing some problems – Antony always maintained that there were advantages in fighting one's battles on one's own ground. Also, he was a member of his uncle's chambers in the Inner Temple; it may not be a good idea to have one's professional activity spill over into one's private life, but there were times when both of them found it convenient. There had been a period of strain at the beginning of the Michaelmas Term, at which time Sir Nicholas and his bride had returned from their honeymoon, when Antony's scruples about continuing to share the house had almost upset the whole arrangement; but somehow or other those scruples had since been laid to rest, and now Vera's presence gave them all a good deal of pleasure.

On Tuesday evenings, by long tradition, Sir Nicholas dined with the Maitlands. Vera seemed happy enough to carry on with the custom, and it was after dinner on one of these occasions that she had tossed her thunderbolt. 'I couldn't have been more surprised if she'd bitten me in the leg,' said Antony to Jenny, when the older couple had gone. 'She isn't usually the sort of person who makes demands.'

'She has involved you in at least four cases in the past,' Jenny pointed out. Seeing that he wanted to talk, she had curled herself comfortably in her favourite corner of the sofa again. 'I don't call that not making demands.'

'But that was a professional involvement, nothing like this.'

'A good deal worse,' said Jenny. 'At least,' she added doubtfully, 'I don't see where there could be any danger in this.'

'Neither do I. But don't you see, love, I haven't a shadow of an excuse for the enquiries I'm going to have to make, and no medical knowledge to help me decide what's true and what isn't.'

'The doctor — '

'Do you think he's going to help me? He signed death certificates for all these people, you know. As far as he's concerned they were natural deaths.'

'Yes, I don't suppose he'll welcome you with open arms,' said Jenny reflectively. 'But Vera is such a good sort, Antony, and Uncle Nick wanted you to go.'

'Yes, and if there's any trouble about it I hope he remembers that,' said Antony, suddenly amused again. 'But I wouldn't count on it, if I were you.'

## WEDNESDAY, 5th January

### I

Jenny was as good as her word, they caught the ten o'clock train the next morning with a quarter of an hour to spare, and were booked into their hotel in time for lunch. Jenny being with him, they'd have taken the car, if it hadn't been for the icy roads. Chedcombe prides itself on its picturesqueness, and reaps the reward of the consequent inconvenience during the summer months when visitors abound. That January day, however, several days before the members of the Bar Mess were due to arrive, they seemed to be almost the only guests at the hotel. The manager himself came out to greet them when they registered; a new man, to Antony's relief. Maitland had always declared himself to be completely innocent as far as the rather dire happenings that followed his first visit to the George were concerned, but the manager at that time hadn't agreed with him, and it was unlikely that he had either forgiven or forgotten in the intervening years.

So they went upstairs and unpacked, taking their time over it, and came down to the dining-room. Here the impression that the place was deserted was shown to be a false one. There was a party of businessmen at the table near the window, and several groups of three or four elderly women disposed about the room. Antony, who had no pleasant memories of his two previous visits to the town, was suddenly inordinately glad of Jenny's presence. If he was condemned to rush in where any intelligent angel would certainly fear to tread, it was at least a comfort to have her to come back to in the evening.

Vera had telephoned her friend Mary Dudley from the Maitland flat the previous evening, and she was expecting

15

him to arrive at her apartment in the nurses' residence at about 3 o'clock. That meant they could have their meal in comfort, but it also meant that Antony had time to get cold feet about the whole business, a fact of which Jenny was perfectly well aware. 'I think I'll come with you,' she said, 'and see what the place looks like. I can always walk back.'

'Better see how far it is first. It's on the outskirts of the town, that's all I gathered from Vera, but I don't really know how far it is from here.'

'If it seems too far I'll come back in the cab,' said Jenny equably. 'What do you really think has been happening, Antony? Something or nothing?'

This was a change for Jenny who always said she hated mysteries. But he had noticed before that any sense of personal involvement in his affairs acted on her like a tonic. 'I don't know . . . Vera doesn't know . . . Uncle Nick doesn't know . . . you're asking me to guess, love. I haven't anything to base an opinion on.'

'When you see Miss Dudley –'

'I shall probably be no wiser. And I know it's a fault in me, love, but I can't feel altogether in sympathy with anyone connected with a place called Restawhile, even if it is masquerading as an hotel.'

'That isn't Miss Dudley's fault,' Jenny pointed out.

'No, of course it isn't.' But then he seemed to have a sudden change of heart. 'I'm not really being open with you, Jenny,' he said. 'Think of the age of these people. I think the whole thing's a nonsense.'

'Then you can tell Vera so, and –'

'Don't say, "Everybody will be happy". I dare say most small towns are gossip-ridden, Jenny, but Chedcombe is one of the worst, I can assure you of that. There are bound to be more deaths in a place where the average age of the occupants seems to be over eighty, and what will the town say then?'

Jenny frowned over that. 'Perhaps the best thing would be if they really were murdered, and then you could prove who did it,' she suggested.

She sounded so serious that he had to smile at her again, though he had rarely felt more distaste for an afternoon's work. 'If one thing necessarily followed the other,' he said. 'But it doesn't, love, you know that.'

When they got up to go, he half expected to hear the rustle of comment that seemed to have followed his every move eight years ago, when first he met Vera, but nothing of the sort happened. Chedcombe had forgotten him, as he wished he had forgotten it. They went out into the hall in silence.

The nurses' residence turned out to be large and ugly, and had been provided by its architect with all the excrescences common to the late-Victorian period. Across the road, the hotel was another matter; a squarish red-brick building, creeper covered, with a good deal of well-polished brass in evidence, and certainly nothing of the institutional about it. An annexe had been built on, with equally formal good taste. At least Antony supposed it was of later vintage; however that might be, the brick was not quite so dark. This he surmised to be the nursing-home wing, and later found that he had been correct about that.

It was pretty cold, but Jenny was well muffled up and decided she would enjoy the walk back to the hotel. 'In that case, I may well get back before you,' said Antony. 'This pal of Vera's is only too likely to send me away with a flea in my ear.'

'Surely after their talk last night – ' Jenny began, and then looked at him more closely. 'You're hoping she will,' she said accusingly.

That was near enough the truth to make him grin at her almost cheerfully. 'I must admit some such thought had crossed my mind,' he told her. 'But I suppose that's too much to expect.'

They parted then, and he watched her as she walked down the street the way they had come. It was odd, he thought, going up the short path to the front door and admiring – as a connoisseur of ugliness – the stained glass that adorned it, that though interviews of varying degrees of unpleasantness were part and parcel of his job, and had been for a long time now, he still looked forward to this coming encounter with a good deal of uneasiness. Even the few additional details that Vera had been able to give him last night had failed to convince him that there was anything at all that needed investigating. If there *was* any funny business going on, that was worse still, because ten to one this matron friend of Vera's was up to her neck in it. And that, he diagnosed as he pressed the bell, was the root cause of his worry. He had always had an affection for Vera, from the days they had first worked together in this very town, and more so now that she was married to his uncle and so much better known to him. It was asking for trouble to meddle in something in which she had an emotional interest; he was sure that ordinarily his uncle would have agreed with him about this, but last night had shown him to be firmly ranged on Vera's side.

She had told him the top floor of the house had been made into a flat for Miss Dudley, but there was only one bell in sight so he rang that and hoped for the best. There was an appreciable pause before the door was opened, rather hesitantly, by a small slight girl; he wasn't immediately sure of her nationality, but she looked darker than ever in her neat white uniform. 'Miss Dudley is expecting me,' he told her. 'I wonder if you can tell me how to get to her flat.'

She was backing away from him, and managed somehow to make the movement graceful. Her smile was both shy and welcoming. 'Mr Maitland,' she said. And then, 'Are you not remembering me?'

He looked at her more closely at that. 'Dera,' he said. 'Dera Mohamad. You must forgive me for not recognising you at once, but I wasn't expecting to meet anyone from Arkenshaw here, you see.'

'I was telling you when we met I would be a nurse,' said Dera simply. 'I have been here now two, three years.'

He was remembering with uncomfortable vividness the last time they had met. Her brother had died in Maitland's hotel room, and although no one had ever been charged, he himself had always been convinced that there had been foul play. But even then, in those tragic circumstances, when she could have been no more than twenty, there had been the same rather touching air of dignity about her. And she seemed pleased to see him, which was surprising; Antony was never one to take credit in his own mind for the delicacy of touch he could display when circumstances warranted it.

'You are coming to talk about these deaths,' said Dera now, surprising him again.

'I was asked – ' said Anthony helplessly, immediately feeling guilty.

'But it is good, are you not seeing that? You will be showing that everything is natural, and then we can be comfortable again.'

'I hope' – and he did hope so, profoundly – 'that you're right about that.' And then, because at the moment this discussion seemed unbearable, he asked quickly, 'The rest of your family, Dera. Are they here in Chedcombe?'

'Still in Arkenshaw. There is Jackie's grave, you see.' (Chakwal Mohamad was the brother who had died.) 'My mother is not wishing to be going far from that.'

'Out of the frying pan into the fire,' he thought ruefully. Definitely, this wasn't his afternoon. 'No, I can see that,' he murmured. 'Dera, we'll talk again, but now Miss Dudley is expecting me.'

'Yes, she is telling me. You will be coming with me, Mr Maitland, I will show you.' She led the way across the highly polished linoleum of the hall and began to ascend the stairs. 'Many, many steps,' she assured him, turning her head and smiling. 'I am hoping you are breathing well.'

'My wife and I live at the top of many, many steps,' Antony assured her. 'So you see, I'm in training.'

Matron's flat was not cut off in any way from the rest of the house; you went up the final flight to what had been the attic floor, and there it was. She must have been listening for them, and indeed their footfalls had been evident enough on the uncarpeted stairs, because no sooner had they reached the top than a door at the front of the house opened. 'Thank you, Dera,' said Matron graciously, and the girl scuttled away as though she were an army recruit who had just been ordered off the parade ground by the sergeant-major. 'You must be Mr Maitland, and I'm Mary Dudley,' she went on. 'You'd better come in here.' He followed her, with a ridiculous feeling that he was entering the lion's den. A nonsensical attitude, he reminded himself, in a barrister of many years' standing, who was entitled to write Q.C. after his name.

The furniture in her living-room was exactly like the house, ugly, over-ornate, but it proved on further acquaintance to be surprisingly comfortable. She did not immediately ask him to sit down, however, but led the way across the room to where a fire was burning in an old-fashioned grate, and then turned to take stock of him. She saw a tall man, perhaps a little thinner than he should have been, with dark hair which was none too tidy, and a casual air that seemed to her to be deliberately assumed. But Antony had been surprisingly near the mark in his estimate of her attitude to his visit. She was grateful to Vera for her concern, though even that emotion was a little grudging. But she resented bitterly, desperately, the fact that she needed help. And this resentment somehow spilled over on to the stranger who had come to ask her questions. So she did not see, as otherwise she might have done, the humorous look about his eyes, or that here was a man whose imagination and sensitivity to other people's problems were in all likelihood the cause of a good deal of distress to him.

Maitland meanwhile, though still wary, could feel his sense of the ridiculous coming to the fore. She was so exactly what she ought to have been, a short tightly-corseted figure, who had probably forgotten how to relax, and of whom he felt sure her nurses were in considerable awe. Her dark hair, like Vera's, was greying, but under her winged cap it was almost painfully neat. The only incongruous thing was her shoes, court shoes with very high heels; much less comfortable, he was sure, than the flat heels that Dera wore, but probably, in the tight nursing hierarchy, a symbol of rank. 'It's good of you to see me,' he said, pushing out the words as tentatively as he might have advanced a pawn when playing chess with a master.

'On the contrary, Mr Maitland. The obligation is all on my side.' That was said stiffly, and his spirits sank again. 'Vera told me you're prepared to go to some trouble on my behalf.'

'So you're obliged to feel grateful to me,' he said, and essayed a smile. She made no answer, only bowing her head as though in agreement, so after a moment he went on. 'I think – I explained this to Vera – that there's very little hope that I can do anything for you. So we'd better not talk about gratitude just yet.'

'Very well.' She moved to a chair near the fire, and waved him to its companion at the other side of the hearth. 'The whole thing is ridiculous, of course. I hope Vera explained that to you.'

'Why is there a problem then?' he asked bluntly.

She did not answer that directly. 'Vera says you've been to Chedcombe before,' she remarked.

'Twice . . . for my sins.'

'Then perhaps you know – ' She left the sentence hanging there, but her questioning tone conveyed her meaning well enough.

'I know enough about the town to realise the force of gossip, once it gets its teeth into a subject. It was because she brought me here . . . a stranger, interfering in *their* affairs . . . that Vera's house was burnt down eight years ago.'

There was a sudden relaxation of her features that with a little effort of the imagination might almost be regarded as a smile. 'I don't think you need take upon yourself all the blame of that, you know,' she told him.

'You've been listening to Vera.' This time he allowed his smile to broaden. 'All the same, I think you can take it that I know a good deal of Chedcombe's capacity for venom.'

'Then I needn't explain that part. What do you want to know, Mr Maitland?'

'Everything,' he said simply.

'But surely Vera told you –'

'Not much . . . really! She only knew what you told her, anyway, and I'm sure you weren't as frank with her as you're going to be with me.'

'I didn't try to hide anything.' The ramrod look was back again.

'No, of course not.' His tone was soothing. 'But you must see that it's important that I hear it from you, then I can ask you questions as we go along.'

She didn't like that. He thought he had never faced so reluctant a witness, and wondered again how he had managed to let Vera manoeuvre him into this position. There was even a puzzle as to why Miss Dudley had confided in her at all, but not knowing anything of their relationship beyond the plain statement that they were friends, he had no evidence to go on in unravelling that problem. 'Where do you want me to start?' she asked, interrupting his reverie, and perhaps a little impatient when she had braced herself for questions and none were immediately forthcoming.

'Begin with the Restawhile Hotel.' But before she could speak he had interrupted himself. 'No, just a minute, Matron, there's something that puzzles me. What are you doing here?'

'My position is that of Matron at the nursing-home attached to the hotel,' she said stiffly.

'Yes, but –' He had been incautious and he knew it. Let it go, and continue with his questions? But unexpectedly she took the decision from him.

'Until I reached retirement age, I was Matron at the Northdean General Hospital,' she told him, and this time her smile was open and quite friendly. 'I could've stayed on, but it hardly seemed worthwhile . . . all that responsibility. But I didn't want to stop work altogether, so when a vacancy arose here in Chedcombe I applied for the position.'

'You've not been here long then?'

It was quite obvious that she wasn't at all taken in by this rather ingenuous attempt at flattery. 'Almost exactly two years,' she said. 'Vera and I are much of an age, you know, though I think she's a few months younger than I am.'

'That explains it then,' said Antony more cheerfully. 'Now . . . we were going to begin with the Restawhile Hotel, weren't we?'

'It's not a name I'd have chosen myself,' said Mary Dudley thoughtfully. He had the impression the remark was made more to gain time than anything else. 'If it was operated by the County Council, you'd call it an Old People's Home. As it is, it's privately owned, but the nursing-home is licensed, of course. The hotel doesn't take anybody under retirement age, but mostly the guests are a good deal older than that. The fees . . . well I can get hold of a tariff for you if you really want to know, but I can assure you it's expensive. It's operated quite independently from the nursing-home, though that's really why we're there; an added inducement to the old people to have some medical aid on the premises when necessary.'

'Vera thought you had some chronic cases.'

'Yes, three.'

'How many beds have you?'

'Eight in all. And during the winter months we usually are pretty full.'

'You don't take anybody from outside?'

'No, only from the hotel.'

'These three chronic cases of yours . . . they're paying guests too, or whatever the proper phrase is?'

'Oh yes, very much so.'

'But it wasn't with them that the trouble lay?'

He had thought she was beginning to relax, but she stiffened again at that. 'The three people who died were all guests from the hotel,' she said.

'Three old people, two of them in their eighties?'

That ought to have encouraged her, but it didn't. She

said, 'Yes,' as though she was admitting to some nameless crime.

'And there was no difficulty about the death certificates?'

'No. Most of the guests at the hotel see our doctor from time to time. Doctor Swinburne had no hesitation . . . this is intolerable,' said Miss Dudley suddenly.

One thing was certain : they couldn't go on like this. 'I'll go if you like,' Maitland offered. And then, assuming a pathetic tone that he hoped might disarm her, 'I'm only trying to help, you know.'

'I know.' She regarded him in silence for a moment. 'Vera had really no right to ask you,' she said then, abruptly.

In a way he would have liked to agree with her; in another, he knew perfectly well that Vera had every right to ask whatever she wished of him. 'I'm very willing to help,' he said, departing from the truth without much pleasure, 'but I can't possibly do so unless *you* help me.'

Mary Dudley thought about that for a moment. 'I can see I'm behaving oddly,' she said at last. 'It's just . . . you know, Mr Maitland, I'm not really used to answering a lot of questions.'

Now that was a sentiment with which he was completely in sympathy. He didn't like answering questions himself. 'I expect being Matron of a hospital is rather like being the Centurion in the Bible,' he said, smiling. 'All the nurses are terrified of you, and rush to obey your lightest whim.'

'Something like that,' she agreed dryly.

'Then . . . shall we go on from there?'

'Willingly.' And that was two of them, he thought, who were telling lies.

'All right then,' he said briskly. 'When did the first death occur?'

'When you say the first death,' said Matron, 'you mean the first one of the three that are causing the talk. Of course, it wasn't the first since I came here. There were two deaths during my first year at Restawhile, but they were both chronic patients and nobody was at all surprised.'

'Why did the town gossips suddenly focus on these three, I wonder?'

'Because, in spite of their age, they were all three people in reasonably good health.'

'But each one was admitted to the nursing-home?'

'Yes. I'd better go back to your earlier question, Mr Maitland. The first death was six months ago, early in July. That was Mrs Reynolds, Anne Reynolds. She broke her hip.'

'But I understand she was a very old lady. Surely in that case – '

'You never knew her.' Again something like a smile disturbed Matron's gravity. 'A redoubtable old lady, quite determined to put up with all the pain and inconvenience and go back to the life she had been living before the accident. She was 89, did Vera tell you that? A good advertisement for Restawhile, if ever there was one. The shops aren't far away, she used to go down quite regularly to the chemist's, or to get her hair done. And she enjoyed a game of bridge, all the best-sellers, and even some of the television programmes, though she was choosy about those. No, I assure you, Mr Maitland, I expected her to get better in spite of everything. And so did Doctor Swinburne.'

'Notwithstanding that, he signed the death certificate.'

'Well, good Heavens, none of us is infallible. Her heart just wasn't as strong as we thought it was.'

'That was the cause of death, was it . . . heart failure?'

'If you want the exact medical terms – '

'Not at the moment.' Time enough to go into these medical mysteries when you were preparing a case for court and it couldn't be avoided. 'But I should like a few more details, please. How did she come to have the accident?'

'She slipped on the steps coming out of the hotel. Such a thing to happen in the summer. And nobody could explain it, but old people's bones are brittle, you know. There wasn't really any need to look very far for a reason.'

'What happened then?'

'She had to go into the hospital, which annoyed her considerably, especially as there isn't much you can do for a

25

person that age except to wait for time to do the work of healing for you. I dare say they would have kept her longer if she hadn't made so much fuss, but after about a week they let her go home again, by which I mean to the nursing-home. We were expecting to have her with us quite a while, you know.'

'What medication was she taking?'

'At the beginning she was under sedation. But no one wants to continue that sort of thing longer than is necessary. If she had asked for painkillers, but she didn't . . . she was a very strong-willed old lady as well as a very brave one. So after a while Doctor Swinburne just gave up the effort. I must say I was glad when he did, because the nurses were having a terrible time with her. After that it was just a question of an occasional laxative, nothing more.'

'You do keep drugs on hand, though?'

'Those that are necessary for our permanent patients, and things that may be needed urgently in the case of sudden illness. That's Doctor Swinburne's responsibility really, everything is kept under lock and key.'

'But you, yourself, and probably some of the nurses, have access to where the drugs are kept?'

'Yes, of course.'

'Well, that's something we can go into later. How long had Mrs Reynolds been back at the nursing-home when she died?'

'About ten days, I think.'

'Will you tell me exactly what happened?'

'She died in her sleep.'

'At what time did this occur?'

'During the night. Even at her age, you'd very rarely catch her sleeping during the day.'

'Who was the nurse on duty?'

'Dera Mohamad, the girl who let you in.'

'Miss Dudley, if it wasn't a natural death . . . what do you think could have happened?'

'Quite frankly, Mr Maitland, I refuse to contemplate any other possibility.'

'In the circumstances the doctor might not have looked any further than what seemed to him to be obvious. I don't think you could blame him.'

'I certainly should not think of doing so.' Well, of course, that was the correct answer, as from a nurse concerning a doctor. But something had given Vera the idea...

'Could any of those drugs you mentioned – ?' he asked tentatively.

'I told you, Mr Maitland, she wasn't on any medication.'

'No, but – ' He hesitated, but no use beating about the bush, after all. 'The suggestion is that she was murdered,' he said then, bluntly. 'That's why I'm here.'

The temperature in the room fell perceptibly by several degrees. 'I think you'd better tell me exactly what you want of me, Mr Maitland,' Miss Dudley said, after a moment.

'If an overdose had been given, of one of the hypnotic drugs for instance, would the doctor's verdict have been any different?'

'Without a *post mortem* there would have been nothing to show, and why should there be a *post mortem* when she had been under the doctor's care? But I think I'd better make it clear to you, Mr Maitland, that I do not allow carelessness. Everything used must be written down and accounted for, even if the doctor is here. And nothing, at any time, has been missing.'

'I see.' He was fumbling in his pocket and produced after a moment a tattered envelope and a stub of pencil. 'That was done after each of the three deaths?' he asked.

'Certainly it was.'

'But there are preparations, I believe, sold over the counter under a proprietary name, that – given in excess – would have a similar effect?'

'I think these questions should be more properly put to the doctor, Mr Maitland.'

'Very well.' He glanced down at the envelope, though as far as Miss Dudley could see the scribbling on it was illegible. 'The next of your old ladies, then, Margaret Henley. Is that Miss or Mrs? A mere youngster of seventy-six.'

'That didn't happen until November. Mrs Henley moved to the nursing-home with an attack of bronchitis, and I wasn't surprised to see her because she had been with us twice each winter since I came to Chedcombe. And, as I am sure you are going to ask me, Mr Maitland, of course the doctor prescribed for her. But nothing that could have harmed her in any way, and again nothing was unaccounted for.'

'Just like the last time.'

'There were similarities.'

'Did they extend to the time of death, I wonder?'

'It happened at night, certainly. She rang for Dera at about eleven-thirty, but when the girl got to her room she seemed to be fast asleep. Dera looked into the room again at about two o'clock, and that was when she noticed that Mrs Henley's breathing was irregular. Half an hour later she was dead.'

'Again with nothing to account for it?'

'Her illness – ' Mary Dudley looked at him and shook her head. 'I expected more scepticism from a lawyer,' she said.

'It all depends which way you look at things,' said Antony. 'Are you going to tell me that the third death also occurred at night?'

'It did. But you must realise, Mr Maitland, that there is nothing uncommon about that. You may think it's an old wives' tale, but the early morning hours are certainly the most dangerous to life in an old, sick person.'

'I'll remember that. Is Dera always on night duty?'

'Five nights a week. But if you're thinking I'm discriminating against her because she's a Pakistani – ' Matron began, no longer ice, but fire. 'She's a very willing girl, and says she likes the quietness of working at night.'

'I never thought anything else. So the second death certificate read, I suppose, "bronchitis", or whatever more exotic description the doctor could think up for it. What did Mr Donald Stewart die of?'

'It sounds ridiculous,' said Matron, relaxing slightly, 'but he got a bad case of whooping-cough. That was about a month after Mrs Henley died. He'd had a cough for days but wouldn't do anything about it. At last, when he was coughing so much he could hardly catch his breath, Mr Williamson, who runs the hotel, positively insisted that he came to me. Even then I had a job getting him to bed, even though I know he thought he was dying. But none of us was very worried about him, not in the long run, that is.'

'And he was taking a cough suppressant, I suppose . . . well, I'll get all that from the doctor. And again he died unexpectedly, and again there was no suspicion?'

'Not until the talk started in the town.'

'When was that?'

'Almost immediately. In fact, I think there'd been some gossip already, after Mrs Henley died.' She paused there, but she obviously had more to say so he didn't interrupt, but sat watching her expectantly. 'I hope I'm not judging the girl rashly,' said Mary Dudley at last, 'but I have always suspected that Hardaker – that's Evelyn Hardaker, my Senior Nurse – went to tea with a friend of hers and talked a little loosely about what had happened.'

'And from that – ?' But he did not try to finish the sentence because he knew only too well how talk could spread in a place like this. 'You've told me a good deal about Mrs Reynolds,' he said, 'and it's hard to think of anybody wanting a gallant old lady like that dead. But what about the other two – were they equally endearing?'

'Mrs Henley was a hard one to please. In her case I don't really blame her daughter for not wanting the bother of looking after her. I suppose I'd call her a shrew, Mr Maitland, if I had to think of a description. But you know, this is all nonsense. If by some coincidence all these people's relations had wanted to get rid of them, how could they possibly have got into the nursing-home at night?'

'There have been cases,' said Maitland carefully, 'where a nurse or a doctor has been venal. You must realise it isn't altogether unknown for such a thing to happen.'

As he expected, that stiffened Matron up again. 'If you have made up your mind, there is nothing more to be said.'

'You don't understand me at all, do you?' said Antony sadly. 'So far I have a completely open mind, but I must admit that the Chedcombe tabbies have this much in their favour, that it's odd that all the deaths occurred in such a similar way.'

'Now you're trying to say that poor child, Dera Mohamad –'

'I'm saying nothing of the kind. Dera is an old friend of mine. But I am trying to find out, first if there is anything to explain or not; and secondly, if there is, what the explanation may be.'

'Yes, I understand.' She sounded subdued now. Despite the fact that she had confided her fears to Vera, Antony wondered now whether she had been really serious about them.

'You were going to tell me about Mr Stewart,' he prompted her.

'Oh, he was another harmless one. Never sick a day in his life, he always boasted, that's why he took so badly to having to come to us in the end. Not a good patient, any of the nurses will tell you that, but a thoroughly nice old man.'

'And they all lived in the hotel.' It was Maitland's turn to sound thoughtful. 'That means, according to what Vera has told me, and what you have told me yourself, that they all had money. Or perhaps had relations who were well-off.'

'I couldn't tell you anything about that, I'm afraid. Mr Williamson, the manager, would be the one to see, he'd know who actually paid the bills.'

'Yes, I'll do that. Can you tell me anything about their relations, Miss Dudley?'

'I can give you the names of their next-of-kin, but no details, I'm afraid.' She got up and walked across the room to an old-fashioned bureau and pulled open a drawer. After a moment's searching she came up with a sheaf of papers, and turned to face him. 'Mrs Reynolds had a nephew, Vernon – her husband's nephew that must have been because his name was the same. And Mrs Henley had a daughter,

Betty; her name is Newbould now, so I suppose she must be married. And Mr Stewart had just the one son, Ian.'

'Have you met any of these people?'

'Briefly. They all called at the nursing-home when first their relations were admitted, and naturally they wanted whatever information I could give them. But as for knowing them – '

'Then that's a matter I must pursue elsewhere. Do you think this Mr Williamson can help me?'

'I'm sure he could, but – '

'You don't want it to get about that enquiries are being made,' he said sympathetically. 'I'm afraid, Miss Dudley, you're going to have to make up your mind, do you want me to continue or not?'

'Vera said – '

'Vera's prejudiced, if you mean about my abilities. I'm going to be frank with you, I don't think there's anything I can do. But if you want me to, I'll try.'

She looked at him for a very long moment. It had been an odd interview, he thought . . . a good deal of antagonism, although occasionally they had seemed to be coming near to understanding one another. Finally she said, 'I trust you, Mr Maitland,' which was just about the last thing he wanted to hear. But it was obviously meant to be the green light, and there was no going back on his promise now.

He came to his feet slowly. 'As Dera isn't on duty, perhaps I could see her now,' he suggested.

## II

Miss Dudley took him downstairs herself, and left him in the big drawing-room, which now had a bleak unfurnished air, while she went to fetch Nurse Mohamad. This, thought Antony, was the interview he ought to be dreading, in view of the circumstances in which they had met before. But then he remembered that she had greeted him without embarrassment, even with friendliness, and he found the recollection comforting.

Dera, when she came in, was still in uniform, and he wondered for the first time why she was wearing it when she was off duty. Perhaps – he allowed himself a certain affectionate amusement at the thought – she was well enough aware of how well it suited her. 'Come and sit down, Nurse,' he invited.

She obeyed him, and was obviously sufficiently relaxed almost to disappear into the big chair. 'Everybody is calling me Dera,' she corrected him. 'I am liking that you will do that too.'

'If that's what you want. Did Matron explain to you why I'm here?'

'Oh yes, she is telling me a little.' But then a thought struck her and she looked at him anxiously. 'There is not being a case in court?'

'Not so far as I can foresee at present. Unless we sue somebody for slander,' he added with unwilling honesty; he had no desire to frighten her at this stage, or, for that matter, at any other. 'But perhaps without that we can put a stop to all this talk that's going on.'

'It is bad, isn't it?' She leaned forward a little, suddenly very much in earnest. 'Is it right that I am telling you something, Mr Maitland?'

'I'm hoping for your help, Dera.'

'But this is something that I am hearing, not because I am wanting to, Mr Maitland, but because I cannot help it.'

'At this stage, that doesn't matter at all.'

'But you will not be thinking – ?'

'I'm quite sure you wouldn't listen deliberately to someone else's conversation.'

'Then I am telling you.' She sounded relieved. 'Matron is thinking that Evelyn is starting the gossip and this I am knowing because I heard her – what is the word? – telling her off about it.'

'Evelyn?' said Antony. He had the name written down,

he was sure. But the sight of him making notes, or even referring to ones he had already made, might alarm her.

'Nurse Hardaker, the Senior Nurse.'

'But you don't agree with Matron about that?'

'No, I am thinking . . . I am certain . . . that it is Shirley Booth who is doing this.'

'Another nurse?'

'Yes, and she is saying — when Mrs Henley died, you know — "that's two of them in a few months. Funny, isn't it?"' That was obviously intended for mimicry, though it didn't come off very well, so he smiled at her.

'Even so, Dera, why should she have repeated it outside these four walls? A rumour like that could injure everybody working here, herself no less than the others.'

'I think it is because she is not liking the place.'

'Why stay here then?'

'You are not understanding, Mr Maitland. It is pleasant work, and it is being much easier than a job in a big hospital.'

'In what way?'

'Not so many patients, one is spending more time with each of them, getting to know them better. Perhaps too there is less — less discipline,' she said, and seemed pleased to have found the *mot juste*.

'I would have thought Matron was a disciplinarian, if ever there was one.'

Dera wrinkled her forehead over that. 'She is with a big hospital before, and I expect she is being like that,' she said 'But with a smaller staff . . . it is not the same, I am telling you.'

'You're confusing me, Dera. If the working conditions are so comfortable that Miss Booth doesn't want to leave, why do you say she doesn't like the place?'

'I am being wrong, Mr Maitland. I should have been saying she does not like Matron.'

'Why is that, I wonder?'

'I cannot be telling you. Matron is always very kind to me.'

He thought perhaps that wouldn't be too difficult, but obviously he must see Nurse Booth. 'Have you any other evidence that she spread the rumours?' he asked.

'Only what she said to me, but that is not until after Mr Stewart, too, is dead. She said then, "They are saying these things go in threes, but I am thinking it is very strange. And Marian when I tell her is thinking that as well." '

'Do you know Marian?'

'Only that she is being a friend of Shirley's who is talking of her often. But, Mr Maitland, how is this helping you? Unless' — she smiled — 'you are bringing that case you are speaking of.'

'I think we'll postpone that for the moment,' he said lightly. 'And you're quite right not to let me get bogged down by inessentials. What I really want to know is anything you can tell me about the nights these three patients died. You were on duty on each occasion, weren't you?'

'I am liking the nursing-home at night,' said Dera simply.

'So I understand. What are your hours of duty?'

'I am there from ten o'clock till six in the morning, Wednesday, Thursday, Friday, Saturday and Sunday.'

'Is there another nurse on duty?'

'Not usually. We are having only three permanent patients. Sometimes in winter when all the beds are being full, another nurse is brought in from one of the agencies.'

'I see. It was summer when Mrs Reynolds was brought into the nursing-home.'

'Yes. She is such a nice old lady. And only four beds full, so I am not needing any help.'

'Did she ever talk to you? About her relations for instance?'

'Oh yes, if she was not going to sleep quickly she was liking to talk. There were friends she was mentioning. No, I am not remembering their names, and a niece and nephew.' She paused frowning. 'Vernon, I think, and Dorothy, but there were their children too that she was talking about. And even a new baby, who would be I think a great-great-nephew.'

'She was on good terms with these people?'

'She is loving them very much.' Dera's tone was a little reproving. 'I am sure she is liking everybody.'

'You said she liked to talk when she couldn't get to sleep at night. Did that often happen?'

'Too often. She is not liking to take medicines, although the doctor is telling her there are things that could not hurt her. So when she is wide awake, I am making her a glass of hot milk. That is never failing to do the trick.'

'The night she died – ?'

'She is already sleeping when I go on duty.'

'No need for the hot milk then?'

'No,' she agreed. She sounded a little doubtful.

'If there's something else, Dera, please tell me,' he urged her.

'She had been having her milk already, there is a glass by the bed.'

'Was it still there in the morning?'

'No, I am clearing it away, of course.'

'Who was on duty before you?'

'That I am not remembering.'

'Tell me, then, what is the routine in the evening in the nursing-home?'

'I am going on duty at ten o'clock,' began Dera a little hesitantly.

'No, I mean before that.'

'Matron is making her rounds at about eight o'clock to see that all is well. And Doctor Swinburne – he is a nice man, Mr Maitland – he is coming every night if there are extra patients, not just those who will always be with us. But, of course, the time is varying, not a fairly fixed thing like Matron's visit.'

'You think, though, that because Mrs Reynolds was in the nursing-home he would have been in to see her that night?'

'It would be unusual if he was not doing that.'

'When did you first realise that Mrs Reynolds was dead?'

'I was not realising it at all. Almost every hour during

the night I am looking in on her, but she is comfortable and sleeping, so I make no disturbance.'

'There was nothing to make you uneasy?'

'There was nothing, Mr Maitland. An old lady sleeping, that is all.'

'Let's go on to Mrs Henley then. She had bronchitis, Matron told me.'

'Yes,' said Dera, and smiled reminiscently. He was rapidly coming to the conclusion that she was tougher than he had thought. 'She is a bad patient, very bad. But of course I am sorry that she is dying.'

For the moment her use of the tenses confused him. Then he realised that she meant only 'when she died'. 'Did she talk to you about her relations and friends?' he asked.

'Only about her daughter and son-in-law. She is not liking either of them very much. Not even her daughter, Betty.'

'And did she also dislike taking medication?'

'Oh, no, no. That is one thing she is good about. I think if the doctor would have allowed it there would have been more medicine used.'

'Did she settle off early for the night?'

'No, she is not liking to settle down before eleven o'clock. There is the telly in her room and something always she is wanting to watch.'

'Did she need anything to make her sleep?'

Again there was Dera's amused smile. 'I am thinking she is not needing anything,' she told him, 'but Mrs Henley is not agreeing with that. Every night I am giving her two of the Drowse tablets that are all the doctor will allow. We are keeping a big bottle in the drug cupboard, for times like that.'

'Then you must have given her something to swallow them with.'

'A glass of water, no more.'

'And this time you did notice something wrong during the night?'

'Her light is going up about half-past eleven. The light that shows when she is ringing her bell. But when I am getting to her room she is fast asleep. I cannot explain it, but it worries me a little.'

'Yes, I can understand that.'

'So every so often I am looking in on her again. At about two o'clock I am noticing her breathing has changed, so I am sending for Matron and the doctor. Matron comes quickly and we are both with her when she dies. Doctor Swinburne comes about five minutes after that.'

'Were you surprised by her death?'

'Surprised, a little. She is not after all very old as compared with most of our patients.'

'Seventy-six,' said Maitland thoughtfully.

'Not very old,' Dera insisted. 'Still, at that age, there is no telling what complications the drugs she has been given will cause.'

It wouldn't be fair to question her about the doctor's reaction; Matron had put him in his place there. 'And it was after that that you heard Nurse Booth making her remarks about the oddness of the situation?' he asked.

'I think she was saying it at lunchtime the next day.'

'And a month later Mr Stewart also died.'

'A nice man,' said Dera, 'but a bad patient. But perhaps that is not surprising. His cough is causing him a good deal of distress.'

'I've never heard of a grown-up with whooping-cough,' said Maitland reflectively.

'He has a cough, he neglects it, it gets worse and worse,' said Dera, with a little, almost pleasurable, drama in her tone. And sometimes it seems as if it is enough to shake him to pieces.'

'And did he, too, need a sedative at night?'

'In his case, it is the doctor who insists.'

'Drowse again?'

'Yes, of course. The doctor says it is so safe, and is not clashing with the other medicines.'

'Safe in the proper dosage?'

'Yes, but always it is the nurse who gives it. Two tablets, no more.'

'What time did he take it?'

'A little earlier than Mrs Henley did, after the ten o'clock news.'

'So again you gave it to him?'

'No, that night it is Matron herself. She is visiting a friend, she said, and so making her rounds late. And he is coughing so badly it is not wondering that she should come.'

'Did he require a drink to swallow the tablets?'

'Yes, but at ten o'clock each night I am taking him a vacuum flask of very black coffee. There would still be some left when I brought him the pills, and he is swallowing them with that.'

By this time Maitland would dearly have loved to be making notes. A barrister's memory is perhaps his biggest single asset, but this was getting a bit too much. 'And did you follow your usual routine of looking in on him during the night?' he asked.

'Oh yes, there is nothing at all to worry about. Only I was a little surprised that he should sleep so peacefully, most nights his cough is worrying him. And the last time I am looking at him before I go off duty, there is something that is strange. He is lying so still and hasn't moved since I saw him before; so I go right up to the bed and I find that he is already dead.'

'And that, as far as Nurse Booth was concerned, was the final straw?'

'Yes, but me, I do not think it so strange. It is a terrible cough, Mr Maitland, and is easily affecting his heart.'

'When you found him, I suppose you called the doctor.'

'Of course I did. He too is not being surprised, Mr Stewart is still coughing badly when he saw him the night before.'

'When was that?' For the first time the question came sharply, and he saw her enquiring look.

'Just after Matron had been, just before midnight.'

'Mr Stewart was coughing then?'

'Oh yes, poor man.'

'Were you with the doctor during this visit?'

'No, because Mrs Cassidy is ringing her bell and I have to go to her. When I am coming out of her room the doctor is just leaving.'

'Then I think the only question that remains is whether Mr Stewart ever talked to you about his friends and relations?'

'He is not talking much because it makes him cough. But there is a son, I know, Evelyn Hardaker has told me.'

'Presumably the son had visited him then.'

'That I am supposing.'

He got up, pleased at the excuse to be on his feet again. 'You've been very patient with me, Dera,' he said.

'And why not? I know you are only wanting to be of help, Mr Maitland. Though I do not see,' she added doubtfully, 'how that can be.'

'So far, neither do I.' He hoped that hadn't sounded too heartfelt. She had risen now and was standing looking up at him, trustfully, he thought, and remembered, to his discomfort, what Matron had said. 'Tell me, Dera,' he added on an impulse. 'What are you really doing here so far from your family and friends?'

'It is not being so far, really,' she told him seriously.

'A cross-country journey, never very easy.'

'Well, there are things . . . my mother and father are wanting to remember, and the others – my brothers and sisters – are younger and must be staying with them. But I am only wanting to forget, so when my training is finished I am going first to Nottingham and then coming here.'

'Poor Dera.' He remembered as he spoke that there had been a man called Tom Bhakkar, about whom she had been in a state of indecision. But all that had been settled within a few days of their meeting by Tom's arrest.

'No pity is needed.' She did not say that reprovingly, but with perfect simplicity. 'I am enjoying my job, and if it is a little lonely, because there are not so many of my people here, still there are some and I am knowing them. As for my parents, it is natural, I think, as one is growing older, to cling to what is past.'

For one reason or another, her words sent a shiver down Maitland's spine. He was a good deal older than this slip of a girl, and he wasn't a man who carried his memories lightly; in fact, he thought, if some sort of selective amnesiac drug could have been found . . . then he realised that she was looking at him enquiringly and hastened to make his farewells.

## III

He spoke to Mary Dudley again before he left, and she promised to rearrange her nursing schedule so that both Hardaker and Booth would be free to talk to him the following morning. She also gave him Doctor Roger Swinburne's address and telephone number, but did not offer to make the arrangements with him herself.

It was already dusk by the time he left the residence, but there was so much to sort out in his mind that he decided the best thing would be to walk back to the hotel and hope that the exercise would stimulate thought. It was further than he thought, but when he arrived he didn't feel that his thinking had been in any way constructive. He was glad to find Jenny waiting for him, curled up with a book in the armchair in their room.

She watched him as he closed the door carefully and came across the room towards the window, and if she noted the stiff way he held himself, as he always did when his shoulder was paining him or when he was particularly tired, she made no comment. That was an arrangement she had made with herself years ago, and after so long it was unthinkable that she should break it. She did say, however, 'Let's go down to the lounge and have a drink'; and if she also thought 'You look as if you could do with one,' that was her own affair.

In spite of the darkness, Antony had been standing looking down into the market square. He said now, 'Let's do that,' but did not turn immediately. When he did it was to smile at her. 'Matron's a holy terror,' he confided.

'Vera's friend?' Jenny was immediately diverted. 'That's not really fair; she ought to have warned you.'

'I don't suppose it has ever occurred to her how my — my intrusion might look to somebody on Miss Dudley's side of the fence. Oh, well, it can't be helped, I suppose. Let's go down and have that drink you were talking about.'

They had the lounge to themselves, which led him to think that the people they had seen at lunchtime had not been staying in the hotel. Here he met an old friend, a waiter who had been elderly even when he had first taken tea with Vera in this very room eight years ago, and wished with all his heart that she had not chosen to sit near the window on a bitterly cold day when she might have taken instead one of the easy chairs by the fire. The old man remembered Maitland, obviously with more affection than the former management did, and had a hundred questions to ask about Miss Langhorne's well-being. It was the first time it had occurred to Antony that his uncle's wedding must have caused a good deal of a stir in Vera's home town; the waiter, he remembered, had always had a soft spot for her, but he would take a small bet, without much fear of losing, that all the comment in the town hadn't been quite so kindly.

But they were alone at last with their sherry. Not the Tio Pepe they drank at home, but 'quite a dry one, sir, we keep it for the gentlemen of the Bar.'

'I hope you're going to tell me,' said Jenny, when the waiter had gone, 'was it a very difficult afternoon?' Jenny had brown, curly hair, that could shine like gold in the lamp or sunlight, and a naturally candid expression, of which she wasn't above taking advantage. Her husband's own word for her was 'serene'; it wasn't very often that he had seen that serenity disturbed. She was also, on the whole, a better listener than a talker, which Sir Nicholas had been known to say was just as well.

Antony was turning the question over in his mind. 'Well, Miss Dudley is in two minds as to whether she wants my help or not, and I don't blame her for that. I suppose you realise, love, that whatever I do will probably only make matters worse?'

'I realise nothing of the kind,' said Jenny indignantly.

'Well, Matron does, or at least that's what she's afraid of. No, really, Jenny, I do think the best thing would be to let the whole affair die a natural death.'

'But Vera thought . . . and she's a very sensible person, Antony.'

'She's asking for a miracle,' said Antony stubbornly.

'When you had talked to Matron – I never can remember her proper name,' said Jenny apologetically. 'When you had talked to her, did you still think there was nothing in it?'

'The coincidence of the three deaths was quite enough to start Chedcombe talking,' Antony admitted. 'But if I'd been the doctor I'd have signed the death certificate all right; there was no earthly reason why he shouldn't.'

'Then it's a shame . . . I mean, it isn't just Matron. There are all the nurses, and the doctor himself.'

'Oh, I agree. That's why I fell in with Vera's wishes in the first place, I suppose. But look at it like this, love : there's no way on earth of proving they weren't murdered.'

'If it was poison they could be exhumed, couldn't they?'

'Not a hope, not on the evidence . . . which isn't evidence at all. No, the only thing that would protect the innocent would be to prove they *were* murdered, and then find out who did it . . . as you pointed out to me earlier. And I haven't a hope in hell of doing that. In any case, do you really think it would stop the scandal?'

'I suppose not,' said Jenny doubtfully, 'but –'

'I agree with you, love, it isn't nice to be on the receiving end of all this scurrilous talk. And I didn't tell you, the night nurse on each occasion was Dera Mohamad. Do you remember Dera?'

'I remember you talking about her, of course, the first time you went to Arkenshaw. She seemed to have made a great impression on you.'

'She's a nice little thing. She has dignity and – and kindness, I think. I should say she's very good at her job, a born nurse. And it doesn't seem to have occurred to her yet, even after all the questions I asked her, that anybody might think she was in any way to blame.'

'That's a good thing, anyway.'

'Yes, but it won't be long . . . we're going round in circles, Jenny. There isn't an answer to the problem as far as I can see.'

'What are you going to do then?' she demanded.

'I promised to see two more of the nurses tomorrow morning, and I know Miss Dudley thinks I'm going to see the doctor too, though I haven't actually said so.'

'In that case you'd better, then you can tell Vera — '

'You've guessed what I was leading up to, love. I'll see him, though I'm not altogether sure of the wisdom of the proceeding. But after that we're going home.'

Jenny heaved a small sigh that might have been one of relief, and for the first time picked up her glass. 'I'm sure Vera will agree there's nothing else to be done,' she said.

'I dare say she will, but what about Uncle Nick?'

'What about him?'

'He knows perfectly well I can't accomplish anything here, but he isn't going to admit it, not as long as Vera is looking for that miracle.' He too began to sip his sherry, and suddenly he smiled at her. 'These newly-weds!' he said.

It was perhaps as well for their peace of mind that neither of them had any idea at that moment how drastically things were to be changed by morning.

## THURSDAY, 6th January

### I

There was a telephone call for Maitland while they were still at breakfast the next morning. He went to answer it, and was gone so long that Jenny sent his kipper back to the kitchen to be kept warm. When he came back he had a frowning look, and did not speak immediately. Neither did Jenny question him, but presently he saw her enquiring look and said in a sober tone, 'That was Matron. There was another death in the night.'

'But . . . Antony!'

'I know, I know. It looks as if Chedcombe has the right cat by the tail this time.'

'Are all the circumstances the same?' Jenny sounded as if she hardly dared to put the question.

'It's another old lady, not one of their regular patients. That's really all I know.' He broke off there while the waiter came back with the remains of his kipper and a warning that the plate was very hot. 'I promised I'd go over as soon as I could, love,' said Antony when the man was gone. 'Though I still don't know what I can do about it.'

'Surely this time the doctor will be suspicious.'

'I imagine so. Oh, well, who lives may learn. Though I'm beginning,' he said consideringly, 'to feel it may be interesting, after all, to meet this Doctor Swinburne.'

Miss Dudley had asked him to go immediately to the nursing-home, and to go straight in, the front door would be open. Inside there was just as much evidence of spit and polish as he had expected, but at the same time it looked far more informal. Matron was there, her back towards the door of what looked like an office, and holding herself even more erectly than she had done the day before, if that were possible. Facing her was a younger woman, not really very tall but looking so in comparison. 'I can't understand it,' she was saying, in a tearful voice, as Maitland went in. 'I had tea with her only a week ago and she seemed so lively then.' (For some reason Maitland thought, Crocodile tears! and then rebuked himself for lack of charity.)

'It was a shock to us all,' said Mary Dudley carefully, 'and I can't tell you how grieved I am at what has happened. Now, my dear, if you want to see the doctor – ' She laid her hand on the girl's arm, and was shaken off impatiently. Matron's colour heightened a little. 'He'll be free in a few minutes,' she added, with no change of tone, 'if you care to go into the waiting-room until he can see you.'

'Of course I want to see him! Where – ?'

'Just across the hall, I'll show you.'

The visitor turned then, and Antony saw at once that she was older than he had expected, in her early forties at least. She said nothing further, took no notice of Maitland standing just inside the front door, but swept across the hall. 'The door on the left,' said Miss Dudley helpfully, and made no attempt to follow. And then, 'Oh, there you are, Mr Maitland,' she went on, sounding relieved. 'Come into my office for a moment, will you?' Evidently his reception today was to be rather warmer than yesterday's.

It was a business-like room, not uncomfortable. She went immediately to the chair behind the desk, as though the very familiarity of it was reassuring. 'Do sit down,' she said absently. And then added, with more humanity than he had expected of her, 'You just about saved my life then; that was Miss Pritchard's niece.'

'Miss Pritchard?'

'The latest victim. That's what they'll be saying in the town,' said Matron bitterly. 'I wonder what you think of us all now.'

'I've no more facts than I had yesterday. If you wouldn't mind telling me – '

'That's why I asked you to come here. I'll be honest with you, Mr Maitland, following the example you gave me

45

yesterday. I don't think you can do anything to help us, but I should appreciate your advice.'

'I need to know what the doctor says. But tell me first, is this a duplicate of the other cases?'

'Not exactly. It's Miss Dolly Pritchard who's died; she had a bad case of influenza and was brought in here two days ago.'

'But again she died during the night, and again – because it was Wednesday night – Dera was on duty.'

'As she works five nights out of the seven, that isn't surprising,' said Matron tartly. But then she relented. 'No, the difference is that Miss Pritchard's heart wasn't strong. The doctor says she could have gone any time. And with the complication of her illness – '

'I see. He means to sign the certificate then?'

'He's determined on it.'

'What about the – the niece I think you said? Is she likely to make trouble?'

'She's shocked, of course. I suppose to her it seems like a sudden death. But when she has talked to Doctor Swinburne I'm sure she'll see things in a different light.'

'You agree with him then?'

'It's a matter in which I must trust his judgement. He was quite convinced everything was above-board in the other cases, so were we all until the rumours started. And even then, I didn't see any reason to change my mind. And this time . . . well, we all knew there had to be special care taken with Miss Pritchard. She's been in here before.'

'Recently?'

'Not since last winter. The same thing then . . . influenza.'

'Is the doctor here?'

'Yes, he promised to come down and see Veronica Pritchard as soon as he'd given the nurses instructions about the other patients. It's upsetting when a thing like this happens.'

'I should have thought – '

'You'd have thought they wouldn't know anything about it,' said Matron, almost humorously. 'You can't keep things to yourself in a small place like this.'

46

'I suppose not. Perhaps I could see Nurse Hardaker and Nurse Booth then, until he's free. Or has all this disrupted your schedule entirely?'

'I told them to stay in the residence, but when this happened . . . they're both upstairs, but I'll relieve them myself in turn and you can talk to them in here.'

'Thank you, Miss Dudley, that will be very helpful. Does Doctor Swinburne know I'm here?'

'He knows. I told him,' said Matron grimly.

'And he didn't altogether approve? Well, I don't blame him. But I wish you'd tell him that if he's willing to see me I shall be grateful, but it must be at his convenience, of course.'

'I'll tell him. Wait here a moment, Mr Maitland. I'll send Hardaker to you.'

Evelyn Hardaker was tall and slim, with dark straight hair very neat under her cap, and rather wide-set hazel eyes. She also had a gentle manner, which surprised Maitland who had been expecting something more bossy. Though, come to think of it, Dera Mohamad was a gentle enough child, so why should he have imagined that her colleagues would be any different?

There were armchairs near the window, and he led the way to those, preferring their informality. He thought Miss Hardaker looked of a nervous disposition and didn't want to frighten her further. 'Did Matron explain to you why I'm here?' he asked.

'Near enough, I think. But there's nothing I can tell you,' she said in a rush, 'except that we were all terribly surprised, even about old Mrs Reynolds. But that doesn't mean we thought anything was wrong. Matron thinks I started all these rumours that are going about, but I didn't, truly I didn't. I wouldn't have said anything even if I'd thought they were true, but I don't.'

That had the ring of truth. 'Chedcombe has always been a place for gossip,' Maitland said, and wondered how many more times he would find that statement relevant. 'But there's this much to be said in their favour, you know, the

47

kind of thing they're postulating isn't altogether unknown.'

'But it couldn't happen here,' said Nurse Hardaker simply.

'Why not?'

'Well . . . there were four different people, if you count Miss Pritchard. Four different families, four different backgrounds. What could they have in common that could make anyone want to kill them?'

'I can't answer that until I know more about those backgrounds you mentioned. But you'll agree it would be possible given the particular circumstances –'

'You're thinking one of us did it!' Evelyn Hardaker gazed at him with horrified surprise.

'You're going too fast, Nurse. I'm not convinced yet that anything out of the ordinary happened. I've talked to Dera Mohamad, you know, but being on night duty she hadn't so much opportunity of talking to the patients. Perhaps you can tell me a little about them.'

'What kind of things?' said Evelyn cautiously.

'Well, were they alone in the world? Did they have visitors?' He'd had a partial answer to this from Matron, but there was no harm in getting another opinion.

'Mrs Reynolds told me she'd outlived all her contemporaries. That's so sad, isn't it? But her nephew and niece used to come and see her, I don't think she was very fond of them though. She always used to tell me that Vernon was her husband's nephew, not really a relation at all. But she enjoyed their visits because she loved having someone to chatter to, I sometimes thought she would have kept me all day talking if I hadn't had other things to do.'

'And Mrs Henley?'

That brought a smile. 'The doctor said "No visitors", and I could tell she was pleased about that. Her daughter, Betty, came one evening with her husband – their name is Newbould as far as I remember – and I came down to talk to them, to explain. And when I went back upstairs I gave Mrs Henley their love as they'd asked me, and she just said, "Stuff and nonsense!" or something like that, as though she didn't like them much. But then I don't think she really liked anybody.'

'Dera said she thought you had seen Mr Stewart's son.'

'Nurse Mohamad is a bit of a chatterbox. But I did see him under the same circumstances . . . I came down to explain that he couldn't see his father. He seemed very disappointed, and I think Mr Stewart was too, but he really was rather ill at the time.'

'You don't know anything personal about these families, something your friends in Chedcombe have told you about them perhaps?'

'I don't listen to gossip, Mr Maitland.' It was a very gentle rebuke, but in the face of it there was nothing more to be said.

'Miss Pritchard — ' he remarked tentatively. It had to be admitted that he was asking the questions mechanically, without much hope of eliciting anything of value. But then something happened that quickened his interest.

Before he could complete his sentence, the door was flung open and a tall, well-built man came in. He was probably in his middle fifties, with black hair greying at the temples, a formidable pair of horn-rimmed spectacles, a straight nose, and a chin with an aggressive tilt that made Antony's spirits plummet at once. 'Are you Antony Maitland?' he enquired belligerently.

'I am, indeed.'

'Roger Swinburne. I don't think you've any more questions to ask Nurse Hardaker just at the moment,' he went on. His eyes never left Antony's face, but Evelyn reacted as though the remark had been addressed directly to her.

'No, of course, Doctor,' she said, and made her way rather hurriedly to the door.

When it had closed behind her, Antony, who had come to his feet — he wasn't quite sure whether it was out of politeness, or in answer to the other man's mood — waited patiently enough to see what was coming next. Swinburne looked him up and down, and said with very little sign of friendliness, 'I've heard of you, Mr Maitland.'

49

That was a remark that Antony always found annoying, carrying as it did a reminder of sometimes unfavourable publicity, but he managed a light tone. 'If you've heard me spoken of in Chedcombe, I don't suppose anything good was said.'

'It wasn't.' Doctor Swinburne laughed suddenly. 'You're not quite what I expected,' he said.

There might be two ways of taking that. 'I'm sorry if my presence here offends you,' said Antony carefully. He thought he could understand the other man's reaction. 'I came hoping to be of help to Miss Dudley, but I'm afraid things have got beyond that now.'

Oddly enough, Swinburne ignored this gambit. 'What's the matter with your shoulder?' he asked abruptly. And then, when Antony made no immediate reply, 'I can see you're in pain.'

If there was one thing more than another that Maitland didn't want to discuss, it was the nagging ache in his shoulder. It was a subject about which anyone who knew him well was aware he was ridiculously sensitive. Sometimes, of course, it was more obvious than at others, and this morning was one of those occasions. It made his movements rather stiff, but that was something he himself knew nothing about. 'I think,' he said, and couldn't quite keep the bitterness out of his voice, 'that is something as little your business as you think your affairs are mine.'

There was a sudden change in Swinburne's manner, he relaxed as though whatever had been troubling him did so no longer. 'Sorry,' he said disarmingly. 'I didn't realise it was something you preferred to keep to yourself, but you know medical men . . . inquisitive.'

'As bad as lawyers then,' said Maitland, accepting the *amende*.

'It was Matron who insisted I should see you, something about taking your advice,' said Swinburne.

'Didn't she tell you beforehand that I was coming here?'

'Yes, of course, but that was before Dolly Pritchard died.

Thought myself you would see it was all a hum, and take yourself back to town.'

'All I have been doing is asking questions at a very superficial level, but I'm afraid the answers haven't made it all that obvious that there's nothing in the rumours.'

'No, but look here!' the doctor expostulated. But then he stopped and obviously rephrased what he had been about to say. 'What is it that makes you suspicious?'

'That's putting it much too strongly. But you'll admit that the number of unexpected deaths – '

'Three in three months.'

'Four now, if you go back as far as Mrs Reynolds.'

'You can't say there's anything unexpected about an old lady of eighty-nine dying?'

'A very lively old lady, according to everyone I've spoken to.'

'And as for Miss Pritchard,' Swinburne went on as though Maitland hadn't spoken, 'her death wasn't unexpected at all. Matron must have told you – '

'Yes, she told me that much, but nothing about the circumstances of Miss Pritchard's death. Were you able to pacify the niece by the way? She was with Matron when I came in.'

'Veronica? She was Dolly's great-niece really. She was a bit upset . . . tell me who doesn't feel that way about a sudden death. But she's not unintelligent, she understood all right when I explained it to her.'

Antony had a private grin for that. 'Were you present when the old lady died?' he asked.

'Yes, I was called in about five o'clock this morning. Matron was already there, with Dera. Dolly was already dead when I arrived.'

'Did you see her yesterday evening?' Dera said – '

'Yes, I make a habit of looking in if we have any patients from the hotel. Last night it wasn't until about a quarter to eleven, and actually that was an extra visit because I had been in around seven o'clock. But I was worried about her condition.'

'Was she already settled for the night at that time?'

'She was awake, if that's what you mean.'

'Had you prescribed anything to make her sleep?'

'If you like I can give you a complete rundown on the medication she was taking.' This time the doctor was obviously irked by the question.

'I was only thinking,' said Antony, with a trace of apology in his tone, 'this stuff Drowse—'

'— is perfectly safe in the proper dosage. Which is why I use it, when necessary. But I would no more dream of prescribing it for a woman in Dolly Pritchard's condition—'

'There have been cases,' said Antony stubbornly.

'Of course there have, that's why we keep it locked in the poison cupboard. But it's perfectly safe in the proper dosage,' said Swinburne again, defensively, 'and all the nurses are quite familiar with it.'

'Well, I don't need the details,' said Antony, thinking it was time to calm the ruffled sea of Doctor Swinburne's temper. 'Though I'd ask for them fast enough,' he added, 'if we were going into court. Even into the coroner's court.'

'There's no question of that. I'll admit, if you like, that an overdose might very well go unsuspected in an old person already ill. But can you imagine what would happen to a doctor who was always crying wolf, always suspecting poison? He wouldn't keep his patients very long.'

'I realise that very well. To tell you the truth, it's been at the back of my mind ever since Vera first talked to me.'

'I wonder what Miss Langhorne thought you could do.'

'She isn't Miss Langhorne any more, you know. She's Lady Harding.'

'Yes, I'd heard something of the kind. But I still don't see—'

'Miss Dudley is a friend of hers, she wanted to help. I'd be the first to admit it wasn't very sensible, my coming here, and I do assure you I see your point of view only too well. But as I am here, and as I have some experience of legal matters, will you let me offer you some advice?'

'You mean criminal matters, don't you?'

'Not necessarily. But if you're so sure, Doctor Swinburne, that Miss Pritchard's death was a natural one, a *post mortem* might go a long way to silencing malicious tongues in Chedcome. And that would be desirable from everybody's point of view, everybody connected with the nursing-home, that is.'

'So that's what you want me to do, is it? Refuse a certificate? I won't do it, Mr Maitland. In a case where I'm sure of my facts it would be most unfair to the family to put them through an ordeal like that.'

'I was afraid you'd say that. You do realise – don't you? – that the talk will be worse than ever now.'

It was Doctor Swinburne's turn to smile, and he did so as though he was really amused. 'If I remember the quotation correctly,' he said. *'They say. What say they! Let them say!* Believe me, Mr Maitland,' he went on more seriously, 'I appreciate what you've been trying to do, and I'm sure your mission here was undertaken with the best of intentions. But we must also remember what they say about the way to hell, mustn't we?'

'In that case, if you're quite determined, I'd better be getting back to town.' Antony spoke with a little more enthusiasm than was, perhaps, altogether polite.

'You don't want to finish your talk with Nurse Hardaker? And Matron mentioned that you wanted to see Nurse Booth as well.'

'In view of your decision, I don't think there's the slightest point in it, do you? But I should like to see Matron again, to make my explanations. And excuses, I suppose,' he said ruefully.

'I'll do it for you, if you like,' Swinburne offered. Maitland only smiled and shook his head. 'Oh, well then, I'll go and find her and tell her she can have her office back. Then I'm going home for an hour or two. To tell you the truth, I could do with some breakfast.'

Miss Dudley had obviously not been very far away. She bustled in before Maitland had had time to decide what he was going to say to her, and her abrupt 'Well?' did nothing to help clarify his thoughts.

'I advised Doctor Swinburne not to sign the death certificate,' he told her.

Matron sat down rather suddenly on the nearest chair. 'Then you do think there's something wrong,' she said. She was jumping to conclusions, but he had to admire the way she treated them when she reached them.

'I didn't say that. I agree with the doctor, there may be nothing but coincidence at work. And in this last case he's so very sure ... that's really why I advised him as I did, you know, because I thought the results of a *post mortem* would set all doubts at rest.'

'Did he agree with you, Mr Maitland?'

'I'm afraid not. He said that it wouldn't be fair to the family, and I can see his point of view.'

'But we can't go on like this.'

He set himself to reassure her. 'I think, you know, that in time the talk will die down. In any case, in view of Doctor Swinburne's decision, there's nothing further that I can do.'

'You don't want to see Nurse Booth, or talk to Dera again?'

'There's really no point in it, is there? I've had some experience of the harm that gossip can do, Miss Dudley, but in this case I can see the doctor's viewpoint as well. And I'm sure that in the long run your own high reputation, and his – '

'We shall neither of us have a shred of reputation left if this goes on,' said Matron unhappily. 'There are the nurses too ... but I can appreciate your position, Mr Maitland.'

'Then I rather hope you'll telephone Vera and tell her so,'

said Antony, with a small attempt at humour. 'Because I'm not at all sure that she'll appreciate it, left to herself.'

Miss Dudley looked all round her, as though her own office had suddenly become unfamiliar. Then she came to her feet. 'I must thank you at least for trying,' she said. And then, preceding him to the door, 'I'm sure you'll be glad to get back home again.'

Jenny was waiting for him. They had lunch at the George, for which for once in his life he hadn't much appetite, and caught the afternoon train to town.


## III

A phone call from Chedcombe before they left had brought a dinner invitation from Vera. Sir Nicholas was already home from chambers when they went downstairs to the study, the room that still got the most use in that part of the house. Vera was obviously full of questions, but was restraining herself nobly; Sir Nicholas poured and served sherry in his usual leisurely way, and then sat down with a sigh of contented relaxation in his favourite chair.

'You're going to have to satisfy Vera's curiosity immediately, you know,' he said then. 'How did your trip go?'

'I think I wasted my time.'

'Don't say that,' Vera begged.

'I'm afraid it's only too true. And there's something you can't possibly know yet, because I don't suppose it would interest the London papers: there was another death at the nursing-home last night.'

That silenced Vera for a moment. Sir Nicholas, after making sure she had nothing to say immediately, turned to his nephew and remarked, 'I dare say I'm being obtuse, but I should have thought that made all the difference.'

'The trouble was, this one had influenza *and* a weak heart. The doctor was even less surprised than he was about the other deaths.'

'But surely – ' said Vera, recovering the power of speech.

Antony did not wait for her to finish. 'I advised him to refuse a certificate, even in those circumstances. If he was as sure as he said he was that it was a natural death, that would put an end to all the talk. But he didn't see it that way.'

'Told you I didn't trust that man,' said Vera.

'I know what you said, but if any of these deaths were contrived we have no reason to suspect him rather than anyone else. He pointed out to me what we both know very well, that no GP goes round making accusations of foul play every time one of his patients dies.'

'And that,' said Sir Nicholas, his eyes now on his wife, 'is reasonable enough.'

'But, Nicholas . . . Mary Dudley! It's a horrible position for her to be in.'

'Again I must agree. Did you reach any conclusion, Antony, as the result of your enquiries?'

'I only talked to Matron, and the doctor this morning, and a couple of the nurses. One of them is Dera Mohamad, by the way; you wouldn't know her, Uncle Nick, she came from Arkenshaw originally. For obvious reasons I couldn't ask questions too near the bone, but I think there is no doubt that any of the nursing-home staff, or of course the doctor himself, could have administered an overdose which would have given the appearance of a natural death. Whether that happened or not, there is no means of knowing.'

'There would have to be a motive,' Sir Nicholas pointed out.

'Yes, but that would mean going into the personal affairs of the four deceased people and their families. In view of the doctor's decision to sign the death certificate, I don't see what good that would do. Except to increase the talk.'

'See that, of course,' said Vera.

'I shouldn't worry too much,' Jenny told her. 'It will run its course and die down; rumours like that always do.'

'Not in this case. Every time there is a death at Rest-awhile – and in the nature of things, with so many old people, there are bound to be some – it will start all over again, whether there are any grounds for suspicion or not.'

Antony got up restlessly and walked to the window and back before he said anything else. 'Tell me what I should have done, Vera,' he asked.

Vera glanced at her husband before replying. 'Think we can agree to differ,' she said then, gruffly. 'We've done so often enough in the past, Lord knows.' And then she added, regrettably, 'Quite sure you did your best.'

Now this phrase, for one reason and another, was one that always irritated Antony intensely, a thing that Vera had not yet learned. Sir Nicholas and Jenny both started to speak simultaneously, both stopped and apologised, but after a little verbal skirmishing Jenny was left in the field. 'I've only spent one night in Chedcombe, but I do see what you mean, Vera, about its capacity for gossip, because I overheard some talk in the hotel lounge this morning, while I was waiting for Antony. But, apart from that, I would like to know, only there doesn't seem to be any way of finding out, whether somebody really is killing these old people, because according to all accounts they were all perfectly happy in their different ways.'

'That's the operative phrase,' said Sir Nicholas approvingly. 'There doesn't seem to be any way of finding out. I really do think, my dear, that your friend, Miss Dudley, will have to be content for the moment with our heartfelt sympathy. She can tell her nurses to answer Antony's questions, though if they refuse I don't see how he can object; and the doctor probably co-operated too, out of courtesy to her. But Antony has no shadow of right to carry his enquiries outside the confines of the nursing-home,' – he gave her one of his sudden, unexpected smiles – 'so I really think that for once in my life I find myself in agreement with him.'

Vera smiled too. 'Must be a strange sensation,' she said dryly. At which Antony relaxed, and went back to sit on the sofa beside his wife. 'See your point, anyway,' Vera went on. 'Nothing to be done about it, nothing at all.'

It was obvious that she was still worried, and obvious

too as the evening went on, that Sir Nicholas to some extent shared her mood. 'But they'll get over it,' said Jenny comfortingly, as they went upstairs later that evening. 'If something else happens, even this Doctor Swinburne of yours couldn't go on being so stubborn. And if there aren't any more deaths I expect it means everything is all right.'

'I seem to have given you the wrong impression about Swinburne,' said Antony, following her through their own front door. But he did not make any attempt to explain his impressions of the doctor more clearly; it had been a long day, and they were both glad to get to bed.

# PART II

# HILARY TERM, 1972

## I

During the days that followed, Jenny was pretty sure that Antony had dismissed Chedcombe completely from his mind. Even on the Tuesday evening, when Mrs Stokes was out and Vera and Sir Nicholas came upstairs for their dinner, he seemed barely interested in the information that Mary Dudley had called, and that there was to be a *post mortem* examination of Miss Dolly Pritchard's body after all.

'I didn't think Doctor Swinburne would change his mind,' he said, placing a sherry glass by Vera's side.

'Could say it was forced on him,' said Vera. 'Woman's niece cut up rough.'

He did take the trouble then to search his memory for the name. 'Veronica,' he said after a moment. 'And I think, to be accurate, she's the dead woman's great-niece.'

'Doesn't matter either way. The thing is –'

'Yes, I know. But the doctor said he'd got her calmed down.'

'All I know,' said Vera. 'Promised Mary I'd tell you. She said you'd be interested,' she added accusingly.

'For Miss Dudley's sake I'm glad, and for the other people concerned too. It should clear things up once and for all, don't you think, Uncle Nick?'

Sir Nicholas took a moment to look from his wife to his nephew, and then raised his glass in Jenny's direction as though proposing a toast to the one person in the room who wasn't likely to disturb his peace that evening. But if he expected an argument to develop, he was wrong. Antony had been out the previous Saturday to buy some new records, and in listening to an account of his discoveries, Vera allowed herself to be diverted.

It wasn't until the following Friday morning that the matter was brought rather violently to Maitland's attention again. Having checked with old Mr Mallory, Sir Nicholas's clerk, to see that his employer was alone, he burst into his uncle's room without ceremony just as the older man was settling down to his morning coffee. 'Do you want me to get Willett to brings yours in here?' he enquired. But his eyes were on the document in his nephew's hand.

'This is no time to be thinking of coffee,' said Antony, with every appearance of loathing. 'I've just been talking to Mallory, and he gave me this.'

'I gather it is something that has disturbed you,' said Sir Nicholas, sipping his coffee with a maddening assumption of unconcern.

'Of course it is! It's a brief from Frederick Byron.'

'Who is Frederick Byron, and why shouldn't he send you a brief?'

'He's a solicitor in Chedcombe, and I met him when Vera and I were defending Fran Gifford.'

'A brief is a brief is a brief,' said Sir Nicholas unimpressed.

'Yes, this one is to defend Roger Swinburne on a charge of murder.'

The coffee cup went down with a clatter. 'The doctor in the case!' said Sir Nicholas, enlightened.

'As you would say yourself, Uncle Nick, precisely. What I'm wondering is, what will Vera have to say about it?'

'Send it back,' suggested Sir Nicholas promptly.

'Uncle Nick, I don't know that I want to.'

'Chedcombe,' said Sir Nicholas, which ought to have had the proverbial effect on his nephew of a red rag to a bull. But,

'I think,' said Antony, rather less than lucid, 'that that's why.'

'If this discussion is to be a protracted one, I shall finish my coffee,' said Sir Nicholas, picking up his cup again.

'And I think you are going to have to explain that last remark, you know.'

Explanations, when he had to make them himself, were a thing that Antony hated. 'Because I know the kind of hell's brew that will have been stirred up there,' he said carefully. 'They'll have Swinburne convicted even before the magistrates' court hearing.'

'Then his lawyers can apply for a change of venue. Whoever they are,' Sir Nicholas added, rather firmly.

'You don't want me to take the case, Uncle Nick.'

'I think Vera will be disturbed if you do. However, you'd better tell me something of the circumstances,' he suggested. 'The *post mortem* results, I gather, were not as negative as you expected.'

'I don't know what I expected!' said Antony, taking a turn about the room. 'Anyway, they weren't negative at all; she had I don't know how much Drowse in her, far more than the lethal dose at any rate.'

'Drowse?' Sir Nicholas was frowning over this information. 'We've come across that before, haven't we?'

'Several times. You don't need a prescription for it, everyone – including Doctor Swinburne – says it's as safe as houses provided you stick to the suggested dose. That's the trouble of course, people don't always do that. And in this case it was kept locked up in the drug cupboard and only doled out cautiously by the nurses if the doctor suggested it. I don't blame anyone at the nursing-home for thinking that was safe enough. But it did cross my mind when I was there that if anything had been used it might have been that; you see, Miss Dudley said all the drugs checked out, but even if Drowse was used from the nursing-home supply, anyone could have bought a bottle and replaced the empty one.'

'It is less than evident, however, why the authorities should have picked on the doctor.'

'I haven't talked to Byron, I don't know anything yet.

63

The magistrates' court hearing is already over, so there's no hurry, I needn't go down till Monday.'

'You needn't go down at all,' said his uncle flatly.

'But Uncle Nick –'

'You're embarking on a crusade,' said Sir Nicholas accusingly, 'and without having the faintest idea whether your client is innocent or not.'

'No, of course, if I come to believe he's guilty I shan't undertake anything beyond the usual exercise of my profession,' said Maitland carefully. 'On the other hand . . . why don't you want me to take the case, Uncle Nick?'

'Because I know the way you work. You've more than half convinced yourself already that this Doctor Swinburne is innocent . . . haven't you?'

'He impressed me favourably,' Antony admitted, 'even though we were arguing most of the time we were together. But what did you mean about the way I work?'

'You'll try to prove his innocence by uncovering the guilty party. Has it occurred to you that your researches may well point to Mary Dudley?'

'She's Vera's friend,' said Antony, as though this presented an insurmountable obstacle to what his uncle was saying.

'Yes, I have the greatest respect for my wife's percipience, but that's still no absolute guarantee of Miss Dudley's innocence. And if any such discoveries are to be made, Antony, I'd rather they were made by anybody but you.'

That took Maitland across the room again. 'I think Vera would understand why I feel I must accept the brief,' he said, coming back to stand beside the desk.

'I'm sure she would. I understand myself for that matter. You can't bear the thought of turning your back on someone who may not be guilty as charged.'

Antony said, 'That's near enough.' And, indeed, it was a good deal too near for his liking. But his dislike of thinking of an innocent man behind bars was a thing that had never been discussed, even with Jenny, not even in the days when the mere closing of a door, let alone the turning of a key in the lock, had made him break out into a sweat. 'I really do think . . . on the face of it there isn't a case to answer, Uncle Nick. So I think I'd better go down there and see what's going on.'

Sir Nicholas gave him a long, hard look. 'I've never had the knack of getting you to change your mind,' he said regretfully. 'But you may as well understand from the beginning, Antony, I will not have Vera upset.'

'That's all very well – ' But then all at once he grinned, cleared himself a corner of the desk, and sat down on it with one leg swinging. 'If it's a matter of preconceived notions,' he said, 'it seems to me you've made up your mind that Matron is guilty. And if she really is, you know, Vera or no Vera, you wouldn't want the doctor to be convicted.'

Sir Nicholas thought about that. 'How right you are,' he said at last with a sigh. 'All the same, I don't like it, Antony, I don't like it at all.'


## II


Maitland went home with his uncle that evening, and stopped for a word with Vera before he went upstairs to his own quarters. With her he was almost as blunt as he had been with his uncle, though nothing was said by any of them about the possibility of Mary Dudley being an alternative suspect to his new client. Vera was looking thoughtful by the time he had finished, though she made no protest when he announced his decision of accepting the brief. Sir Nicholas remained carefully neutral, to his nephew's annoyance – which was illogical – but he sat up with a sudden display of interest when Maitland concluded,

'I think you understand my motives well enough, Vera. What about coming out of retirement and joining forces with me?'

'Are you actually suggesting – ?' asked Sir Nicholas outraged.

'Just what I say, Uncle Nick.'

'Don't need a junior to go special these days,' Vera told him.

'I know that.' And she knows that I know it, he thought rebelliously. 'All the same, Vera –'

'Besides, no brief.'

'On the contrary, Byron specifically mentioned you to Mallory. I didn't tell you that, Uncle Nick.' Sir Nicholas gave him a long look, but made no comment. Vera was continuing with her protestations.

'Know perfectly well I've got my doubts about this Doctor Swinburne of yours.'

'Have you ever met him?'

'N-no,' she admitted, as though unwillingly. The slight hesitation was very unlike Vera.

'Then your opinion of him must be based on what Matron has told you.'

'Mary wouldn't criticise him.' Vera gave one of her rather grim smiles, which – in the earlier days of their acquaintance – had alarmed him considerably. 'It wouldn't be at all the thing.'

'All the same –' he insisted.

'Something of the sort may have been apparent in her manner,' Sir Nicholas suggested, 'without anything actually being said.'

'Expect that was it,' his wife agreed with an air of relief.

'Do come, Vera,' Antony urged her. 'You can keep an eye on my activities,' he added, glancing sideways at his uncle as he offered the inducement. But Sir Nicholas for once was not to be drawn.

'What are you proposing, Antony?' Vera wanted everything in black and white. 'Do you mean to involve yourself beyond studying your brief and appearing in court?'

'I mean to go down to Chedcombe and – and do whatever seems to be necessary,' he told her.

'And if you decide your client is guilty?'

66

'Who am I to judge? But you know the answer to that, Vera, I shall proceed exactly as you outlined.'

'But if you decide he's innocent, you'll go all out to throw the blame elsewhere?'

'How well you know me.' He glanced at his uncle, but Sir Nicholas declined to meet his eye. 'There are all sorts of possible angles, but I shan't know anything until I've talked to Byron.'

'I should like to be present at that meeting,' said Vera, suddenly relenting.

'Well, why not? It will only be for a day or two, and Jenny will look after Uncle Nick for you. And then we'll have to go down when the case comes on, of course, but still –'

'Pray do not allow any consideration for my comfort to interfere with my nephew's whims,' said Sir Nicholas silkily.

Vera gave him a look that for one moment was a startled one. But she was almost as good now as Antony and Jenny, with their years of experience, at deciding whether her husband was serious or not. In this case, of course, as Maitland knew well enough, Sir Nicholas's remarks might be regarded as an enthusiastic endorsement of the plan.

'All right then,' said Vera, making up her mind. 'I'll come with you, but not for more than a couple of days, mind. And if you get any particularly outrageous ideas into your head –'

She didn't attempt to finish the sentence, but Sir Nicholas summed up her meaning for her well enough. 'I shall be sorry to lose your company, my dear,' he said. 'But you don't know what a weight that will be off my mind.'

## MONDAY, 17th January

## I

After some further consideration it was decided that they should go down on the early train on Monday. As the Crown Court was now in session there was no question of Jenny accompanying them – with the members of the West Midland circuit gathered at the George that would have been considered too eccentric by half. The weather had relented a littie, in that it had grown a good deal warmer, but though it wasn't actually raining, the air felt damp as they came out of the station, and Maitland looked round for a taxi. 'I shan't be sorry to get some lunch,' he said, as they embarked on this last leg of their journey. Vera had been ominously quiet all the way down, and though she was never a great talker this had worried him. He felt that a meal, and perhaps a good stiff drink to precede it, might do her good.

Either one or the other did the trick. Over their coffee she confided in him that she was still worried about Mary Dudley. 'Haven't let her know that I was coming,' she said. 'Awkward, if she knows I'm here. But if she's a prosecution witness – '

'We'll know when we've talked to Byron,' said Antony. He could see her point, and having got his own way was inclined to be sympathetic. 'He said to go across to his office as soon as we finish lunch, so you shouldn't have too much longer to wait.'

It was drizzling gently when they strolled across the square to the solicitor's office. The elegant grey stone house was changed hardly at all, except that the brass plate now displayed the words FREDERICK BYRON, SOLICITOR AND

COMMISSIONER FOR OATHS; the first Byron's name and that of Tommy Davenant having disappeared. And inside, as before, the hall had a faintly battered air, though the linoleum had been well waxed. But nobody had repainted the walls, a hideous shade of chocolate brown below, and a depressed and indeterminate biscuit colour above. Maitland's spirits dropped several notches, but Vera, to whom the place must have been much more familiar, behaved (so he thought) rather like a war horse scenting battle. She charged without ceremony into the general office; it was a different girl there, since Antony's time, but she seemed to know Vera well enough. 'Mr Byron's expecting you, Miss Langhorne . . . Lady Harding,' she said, and turned a smiling look on Antony. 'And Mr Maitland too, of course.'

Frederick Byron had kept his upstairs office, the best room in the house as a matter of fact, as befitted one who had been in his day the senior partner. It was a big room overlooking the market square with comfortably shabby furnishings. Byron, by Antony's reckoning, must be in his early sixties by now. You couldn't call him fat, 'portly' was the word that came to mind, but he had to admit that the solicitor had put on a certain amount of weight since last they met. He was a tallish, dignified figure, immaculately turned out. His fair hair was still thick, and waved in an orderly way that had once aroused Antony's envy; for the rest, he had rather a ruddy complexion, regular features, and vividly blue eyes.

But none of this registered particularly on the visitors. Byron was too familiar to Vera; and, as for Antony, he was largely preoccupied with his own feelings. The memory of that last meeting, like so many of his memories of Chedcombe, was not a pleasant one. Not that it had been in any way unfriendly . . . just that Byron was one of the people he would have preferred not to meet again, since he had been instrumental in bringing home a rather nasty series of murders to his partner. But if Byron remembered anything of this, as, of course, he must remember, there was nothing to show it in his manner. He greeted Vera first, like the old friend she was, and then turned to Maitland. 'The last time I asked you to act for a client of mine you refused, for a very good reason. I'm glad you could see your way to agreeing this time.'

'The circumstances are rather different,' said Maitland, waiting till Vera had seated herself and then taking the chair to which Byron waved him. 'But I wonder,' he added bluntly, 'why you didn't brief some member of this circuit. Why me?'

Frederick Byron had gone back to his own chair behind the desk. Now he clasped his rather plump hands on the blotter in front of him, and seemed to be giving the question rather more attention than it perhaps deserved. 'For the same reason, I suppose, that Vera insisted on your being brought into the Randall affair,' he said at last.

Antony smiled at that. 'She had some qualms about it later,' he admitted. 'Still, here we are, completely in the dark except as to the fact that our client has been arrested.'

'That's easily remedied. Did you know Roger Swinburne, Vera?'

'Never met him. Most of his practice is in the same district as Restawhile, other side of town.'

'I thought perhaps . . . you were a friend of Mary Dudley, weren't you?'

'Still am.' That was Vera at her gruffest. 'Nasty business, all this. Glad to get to the bottom of it.'

'That's exactly how I feel.' He turned to Maitland again. 'And if anybody can do it – '

'I shan't be able to do a thing unless you give me the facts,' said Maitland, a little tartly. 'For instance, there were three deaths that caused talk, but when I saw Swinburne he was perfectly sure the fourth one was natural. As sure as he had been in the previous cases, of course. Now I understand that the niece, Veronica Pritchard, kicked up a fuss,'

'She certainly did. Well, you know the procedure as well as I do. There was nothing for it but a *post mortem*.'

'And that uncovered the fact that she had had an overdose of that sleeping stuff. What are they doing about the other three deaths?'

'Nothing,' said Byron blandly.

'But that's insane! Anyway . . . when I was down here before I wasn't at all sure that there had been foul play, you know, but if there had, any one of a number of people could have done it. So why, in heaven's name, why the doctor?'

'That's an easy one to answer,' said Byron. 'Dolly Pritchard was a wealthy old lady. She made him her sole heir.'

That brought a silence. Maitland didn't dare look at Vera, though he was aware of her heavy breathing beside him; it seemed only too likely that she was thinking something on the lines of 'I told you so!' After a while he said slowly, 'Am I right in thinking that's why the niece wanted the *post mortem*? Did she expect to inherit?'

'Spite,' agreed Byron, shaking his head sadly. 'Just spite. But perhaps we shouldn't blame her too much for feeling disappointed. She's engaged to be married –'

'Who is the man? What does he do? Is he in need of money?'

'Don't get excited,' Vera advised him. 'Everybody is in need of money these days.'

'Yes, of course; but I meant, has he any specific need?'

'I know very little of the young man,' said Byron, his tone disclaiming all responsibility. 'I've no doubt the information is available, however, if we dig for it.'

Maitland very nearly retorted that that ought to have been done already. He stopped in time, and said only, 'The other deaths?'

'Are being written off as natural, and when you talk to Roger Swinburne you'll find that's what he himself believes.'

'Yes, I know, he told me that.'

'As for the police . . . well, you see, *they* didn't leave Roger any money, so where's the motive?'

'That, if I may say so,' said Maitland, coming to his feet, 'is a very poor argument. It's presumed they all had money, as they were living in an expensive hotel –'

'Might have been annuities,' Vera put in.

'Well, yes, so it might. But let's suppose for a moment that they had money to leave. Somebody got it.'

Byron's eyes followed him meditatively as he took a turn about the room. 'Is that the line you're proposing to work on?' he said at last.

Antony came back to stand behind his chair. 'In the circumstances, I don't think the alternative would appeal to our client,' he said.

'And that is?'

'To say it was a mercy killing. Of course he'd have to deny all knowledge of the legacy.'

'He does that anyway.'

'And I don't see our getting away with that, do you?'

'Difficult,' said Vera.

'In any event,' said Frederick Byron at his most dignified, 'my instructions are to plead Not Guilty.'

'So I supposed, but we've got to put all the options in front of him.'

'And if he refuses to consider that one – ?'

'Then we'll have to play up the other cases for all they're worth . . . show method, if that's possible. Because our client had no shadow of motive there.'

'Nor had anyone else,' Vera reminded him dryly.

'We're postulating a financial motive . . . remember? People can get awfully weary waiting for dead men's shoes.'

'But, my dear Mr Maitland, none of these people would have had the opportunity,' Byron protested. 'And they're all well known in the town; very respectable people.'

Vera grimaced at that, as though she knew how her nephew-by-marriage would take it. Antony said, '*That* doesn't reassure me.' And then, 'As for opportunity, I think

72

we're assuming some obliging member of the nursing-home staff, aren't we?'

'Nobody,' said Byron, in a much less robust manner than was usual with him, 'could possibly be so wicked.'

'Don't you think so? It's been done before, and no doubt it will be done again. And certainly your neighbours in Chedcombe here have no difficulty in believing it.'

'Interesting point,' said Vera. 'What are they saying now?'

'They've forgotten all about the first three deaths, and are concentrating all their malice on Roger Swinburne,' said Byron. 'Which brings us to a rather important question. Do you want a change of venue when the trial comes on?'

Maitland consulted Vera with a look, but her expression was not illuminating. 'Give us a day or two to think it over,' he said then. 'When our plan of campaign begins to take shape . . . by the way, will Mary Dudley be giving evidence for the prosecution?'

'I suppose you wanted to see her, Vera,' said Byron. 'Well, I'm afraid she's their witness, so it won't be possible. I've got all the statements, of course.'

'Could at least express my sympathy,' said Vera. But then, before either of her companions could comment on that, she added, 'Not at all wise, in the circumstances.'

Maitland thought that perhaps she was taking comfort from the idea that he couldn't question Matron either, until they got into court. 'And Dera Mohamad is out of bounds too . . . well, obviously they'll call her. Who else among the nursing staff?'

'The Senior Nurse, Evelyn Hardaker.'

'And no one else?'

'I think the idea is that Mohamad and Hardaker are the two nurses who hold keys to the poison cupboard. Of course, they hand them over when they're not on duty, but the little Pakistani girl was on on the night Dolly Pritchard died, and Nurse Hardaker had been on duty during the day.'

'I see. Not that it matters much, because as far as I can

73

see anybody, anybody at all, could have administered this wretched stuff. I'd like to see Nurse Booth if I can,' — Frederick Byron was making notes now — 'because she's the one that Dera said started all the gossip. Otherwise I think our enquiries will be more useful outside the nursing-home, so if you can arrange for us to see the surviving relatives of the victims —'

'You're getting ahead of your data,' said Vera.

'So I am. The relatives of the three people about whom there was originally some speculation,' Maitland corrected himself. 'Veronica Pritchard — the niece's name, isn't it? — is obviously off limits too, but perhaps we could talk to her *fiancé*.

'That could certainly be arranged, I think. His name is Bill Sanders,' said Byron helpfully.

'I suppose he's a respectable member of the community too,' said Maitland in a depressed tone. 'You never answered my questions about him, you know.'

'He's an architect, a brilliant chap by all accounts. There was some talk about his being made a partner in the firm he works for, but I heard he couldn't come up with the necessary capital.' Byron, a Chedcombe man bred and born, quite obviously put a different interpretation on the words 'very little' from the rest of the world.

'Doesn't mean he'd arranged to have an old lady killed to get it,' said Vera in her gruffest tone.

'That, I assure you,' said Byron a little huffily, 'was the furthest thought from my mind.' But Maitland was following his own train of thought.

'How old is this paragon?' he asked.

'He was at school with my nephew, so that means he must be . . . oh, say in his middle thirties now.'

'And Veronica is every day of forty. Perhaps a little more.'

'Not enough difference to matter,' Vera told him.

'That wasn't what I had in mind. I was thinking . . . well, it doesn't matter. When can we see Swinburne?'

74

Byron glanced at his watch. 'I arranged it for four-thirty,' he said, 'so by the time we've driven out to the prison – ' He did not attempt to finish the sentence, but got to his feet as he spoke. Antony, already standing, turned rather reluctantly now towards the door. Of all the matters he dealt with, this was the part he hated most. A visit to a client already under lock and key, with freedom only a memory. And because he did not want to think about that, he raised the question again, 'I can't think why you wanted to send for me.'

'But I told you!' Byron was inclined to be querulous. 'Besides,' he added, 'it was Roger's suggestion in the first place, though I admit I thought it a good one.'

'That only makes it all the more incomprehensible,' said Maitland, and this time reached the door and pulled it open. 'I didn't think our client was loving me much when last I saw him, you know.'

## II

The prison had been built well outside the town, so as not to disturb the atmosphere which the summer visitors found so attractive. The authorities had been wise in that, Antony thought, as they arrived; a hideous building, for a purpose no less hideous. He caught Vera's eye for a moment, before she turned to follow the warder, and surprised a look of unmistakable sympathy; uncharacteristically, his lips were set in a narrow line as he fell into place in the little procession.

There was only one introduction to be made when Doctor Swinburne joined them, under guard, in the interview room. He was very pale, as though prison life even in this short time had affected him, but he had himself pretty well in hand. In fact – Antony's thought was tinged with the humour that with him was never very far away – he was considerably calmer now than he had been when they met at the nursing-home. When the doctor had been made known to Vera, and the door was locked again with the warder outside, they found themselves chairs round the long bare rather dusty table. Roger Swinburne chose a seat with his back to the door; Vera, who knew Antony's ways, manoeuvred him to the opposite end of the table, seating herself on his left side and leaving Fred Byron no option but to take the one remaining chair. Maitland, as usual when the going was difficult, longed to be on his feet; but the first thing was to establish some rapport with his client, so he fished in his pocket for one of the envelopes he had put there before leaving home, and for the stub of pencil he preferred. He had lost count of the number of propelling pencils he had been given from time to time, but he always broke the lead when he got rattled, and as soon as that happened they were consigned to the drawer of the writing-desk and forgotten.

Byron was talking to his client. 'You see, I was able to comply with your wishes and persuade Mr Maitland to come here,' he said. 'Lady Harding, as I dare say you know, has worked with him before. You couldn't wish for a better team.'

Roger Swinburne answered that with an inclination of his head, first in Vera's direction and then in Antony's, but it was to the latter that he spoke. 'I didn't think I'd be seeing you again so soon,' he said.

'I'm sorry,' said Antony formally, 'that it should be under these precise circumstances. Now, I'm probably going to weary you with questions, but there's one thing I should like to know first of all.'

'Whether I killed her,' said Swinburne militantly. 'Well, I didn't!'

'That wasn't what I was going to ask you. I have my instructions from Mr Byron, you know, and he told me the plea is Not Guilty.'

'But still you'd like to be sure. I know all about you, Mr Maitland –'

76

'Oh?' queried Antony gently.

'I'm sorry, that was a silly thing to say. But I do know enough to realise that you won't launch an enquiry into what's been happening unless you believe what I say.'

'All right then, convince me! But first there's this question.'

'What is it then?'

'The first three deaths, the ones that started all the talk. What do you think about them now?'

Swinburne considered. 'That's a difficult one,' he said at last. 'I was so sure in my own mind that it's hard to reverse my decision. But naturally, Dolly Pritchard's death — about which I was even more certain — having turned out to be murder, that makes a difference.'

'I think it does. I think it makes all the difference in the world. And that's something that may prove very important to you, Doctor, whether you realise it or not.'

'In what way?'

Antony explained, very nearly in the words he had used earlier to the solicitor. 'Mr Byron tells me there is no question of exhumations,' he concluded.

'Well, I'm not in a position to demand them. If you could persuade the next-of-kin . . . after all, it was Veronica Pritchard's doing that the *post mortem* was done on her aunt.'

'I shall try to do that, of course, but I haven't much hope of success. But before we go on there's another thing we must be clear about : were you remembered in even the smallest way in any of these people's wills?'

'No, I wasn't.' Swinburne was scowling now.

'Well, that's something to be thankful for, at any rate.'

The doctor was following his own train of thought. 'I suppose you think I've been very blind,' he said, 'not seeing what was going on under my nose.'

'We don't know yet that anything was going on.'

'But, as I told you, I'd never in my wildest imagination

77

thought of such a thing. If I'd had the faintest idea . . . heavens, man, I'm here to save lives not to take them.'

'In that case we'd better get back to the specific charges against you. Unless . . . have you any questions about the other deaths, Vera?'

Vera had been silent for so long that her deep voice seemed to startle the prisoner when she spoke. 'Covered everything,' she said. 'Can quite see how it happened, too; no doctor in general practice goes about expecting the worst.'

That was a long speech for Vera. Swinburne might be alarmed by her gruffness, but Maitland recognised with amusement the first signs that her opinion of the doctor was changing. As for himself, that would have to sort itself out later, if it was to sort itself out at all. Byron seemed to believe in his client, but they were probably old friends. If the man had not been so determined on signing that fourth death certificate . . . 'The matter of Miss Pritchard's death,' he said firmly, the firmness as much to call his own thoughts to order as for any other reason.

'I've already given Fred Byron complete details of the treatment she was having,' Swinburne told him.

'Yes, well, that's something I'd rather study at leisure. The first question I had in mind is what sort of person she was. I've talked to you, and to Matron, and to some of the nurses, and all the patients seemed to be referred to as Miss or Mrs So-and-so, even Mrs Reynolds, whom everybody seems to have loved. But Miss Pritchard is almost invariably Dolly. Why is that?'

'Well, she was a very jolly old lady, with no time for formalities. But besides that . . . you don't know who she was?'

'Should I?'

'She was before your day, of course, before mine, too, for that matter. But in her heyday she was very well known indeed as a musical comedy star.'

'So that's how the milk got into the coconut!' Antony

said. Vera scowled at him, which he considered unfair; she wasn't above using colloquialisms herself. 'I mean,' Antony corrected himself, 'that's where her money came from?'

For some reason this unconventional remark on the part of his counsel seemed to have raised Doctor Swinburne's spirits. 'She made a pile,' he agreed. 'And if your next question is going to be, why she left it to me, I haven't the faintest idea.'

Antony got up. He'd been sitting long enough, and besides the situation was beginning to irk him. 'I'm afraid we can't just leave it there,' he said. 'For instance, supposing Miss Pritchard's death had turned out to be a natural one, would there have been any grounds for her niece suing you for undue influence in the making of her will?'

That, as he had expected, put the cat back among the pigeons again. 'There could have been no evidence that I tried to influence her,' snapped Roger Swinburne, 'because I never did.'

'Can you explain then why she should have singled you out in this way?'

'I can't explain it, I don't know.' His anger had died now, he sounded both helpless and hopeless.

'Let's get at it another way then. What were your relations with her?'

'She was my patient for the last three years, and I like to think my friend.'

'That was the time she had been in the hotel?'

'Yes. I explained to you about her heart condition, that meant that I saw her regularly. But she never gave me the faintest hint . . . believe me, Maitland, I had no idea!'

'You did, however, spend some time in conversation with her, perhaps more than you would with an ordinary patient?'

'That's true enough.' He smiled, as though at some pleasant recollection. 'She was interested in everything, I think, and you know old people can get very lonely.'

'She had never married?'

79

'No. That isn't to say there may not have been some — well, some irregular relationships when she was younger.'

'I think I get the picture.' Maitland was smiling too. 'So now she was alone in the world, except for this niece, Veronica Pritchard?'

'Ronnie, yes. But we should be saying great-niece. Her brother Edward's grand-daughter.'

'Her nearest relative?' Maitland insisted.

'Her only relative, as far as I know.'

'You called her Ronnie. I take it you knew her too.'

'Not so well as I knew Dolly, of course, but I met her from time to time when she was visiting Restawhile.'

'Did she do that often?'

'With what I suppose you could call regular irregularity,' said Swinburne, obviously thinking it out as he spoke. 'She told me once as we left the hotel together that it wasn't fair to get Auntie to expect a visit on any particular day. So she made it a habit to vary her times of coming.'

'I suppose that's reasonable,' said Maitland, not altogether convinced. 'What do you know about her?' He divided the remark equally between solicitor and client. 'What had Chedcombe got to say about her?'

'She's a teacher at Rosedale, that's the girl's boarding school on the outskirts of town. I seem to have heard — it must have been from Dolly — that mathematics is her subject. And I have never heard any talk about her — have you, Fred? — so I suppose that must mean her reputation would stand inspection.'

'That's my impression, too,' said Frederick Byron. 'Actually, I'd never heard of the woman until this business came up.'

'So that brings us to her relationship with her aunt . . . great-aunt. Though it would be simpler to forget the "great" for the time being, don't you think?'

'Much simpler.' Swinburne was frowning again. 'I can't say I've ever given the matter any thought before,' he said, 'they seemed on good enough terms when I saw them together, and if there was any friction Dolly wasn't one to complain.'

'Do you think Veronica expected to inherit?'

'I think it would be a reasonable expectation. *I* certainly expected her to do so.'

'If Miss Pritchard were annoyed with her niece for any reason, do you think she might have made the will in your favour out of spite?'

'No, I don't.' The doctor's tone had sharpened. 'I don't believe Dolly had a malicious bone in her body. But if she decided for some reason or another that she didn't want Ronnie to benefit, she might quite well have named me her heir because we were good friends. She was well into her eighties, you know, and she told me once that most of her contemporaries had predeceased her.'

'I see. That sounds very reasonable' He paused a moment, his eyes were on Vera, though he was not seeing her. Then he quickly turned back to his client again. 'What do *you* think of Veronica Pritchard?' he asked.

Again Swinburne took his time about answering, and when he did speak seemed not altogether comfortable. 'I didn't like her,' he said at last. 'I thought she was a hard woman, but there's no way she could have given her aunt the overdose, you know.'

'I thought you understood, Doctor. We shall base our defence on the four deaths, not one.'

'I still find it hard to believe —'

'For your own sake you'd better have a shot at it. Six impossible things before breakfast,' said Maitland vaguely. 'You didn't like Veronica Pritchard. Do you suppose she liked you?'

'That's something else I never thought about before. I should imagine she was pretty indifferent to me really.'

'When I saw you last week you told me she was shocked by her aunt's death, but you thought you had got her calmed down. What made her change her mind and demand a *post mortem*?'

'That's only too obvious, I'm afraid.' Swinburne sounded genuinely regretful. 'It wasn't until she discovered the contents of the will. That gave her extra ammunition of course; she might not have been listened to without that.'

'I suppose she felt at that point that she had nothing to lose,' said Maitland. 'You'll agree *she* at least was motivated by spite,' he added, as though the idea somehow cheered him.

'I think that's fair enough. Not that I care for the idea much myself,' he added, as though his counsel's attitude puzzled him.

'Never mind that, let's forget her for the moment. The night your friend Dolly Pritchard died, Doctor. What do you remember about it?'

'I told you—'

'I haven't forgotten. But I shall need a little more detail.'

'Well . . . I've always made it a habit to call in at the nursing-home in the evening, if any of the residents of the hotel were there. Or if any of the chronic cases needed an extra visit, of course, but at the moment they're all pretty stable.'

'Just a minute! Was Miss Pritchard the only patient from the hotel?'

'Yes, though I didn't expect she'd be the only one for long. Flu generally goes through the old people pretty quickly. Anyway, as I was saying, I went in about seven o'clock in the evening, and I wasn't too happy about her. She had all the usual aches and pains, and her breathing wasn't too good. That could have been dealt with; it was her heart I was worrying about.'

'So much so that you made a second visit later that evening?'

'Yes, I did.' He sounded on the defensive now. 'About a quarter to eleven. I didn't notice the time exactly, but it was five to when I left the nursing-home. She seemed a little better. Do you want me to get technical about this?'

'Not at the moment. Go on.'

'That's really all. We chatted for a few minutes, and then I left.'

Antony exchanged a glance with Vera. 'That's only half the story,' he complained. 'For instance, were you alone with Miss Pritchard? Which of the staff did you see when you were in the nursing-home? And how do you think the overdose was administered?'

Doctor Swinburne looked a little taken aback by this comprehensive demand. 'The only one of the staff I saw – and I suppose that's what you mean – was Dera Mohamad. She – '

'I know Dera. That's another thing: even Matron, who normally addresses her nurses very formally, always calls her by her first name.'

'You mean, in the same way that Dolly was always Dolly? I suppose because she's such a friendly little thing. You say you knew her before?'

'Yes, I met her when she was still living at home in York-shire. That's beside the point, Doctor. What about my other questions?'

'I saw Dera on the upstairs landing, she was busy with some records at the desk there. I told her why I'd come, and I think normally she would have accompanied me, but at that moment Mrs Chester's bell rang and she had to go to her. So I was quite alone with Dolly, and had every oppor-tunity – '

'Yes, you needn't rub it in. This Drowse stuff, I've met it before. It's odourless and tasteless and easily soluble. What did Miss Pritchard normally drink at night?'

'She was on a liquid diet, but she couldn't stand milk, which made it rather trying. I expect she had some earlier in the evening, camouflaged in some way . . . Ovaltine, Horlicks, something like that. But what she did like was orange juice, and there was always a jug by her bed, and a glass, of course. If someone wanted to hurt her, which I still find hard to believe, there were the means already to hand.'

'I'll say this for you, Doctor, you take a good deal of convincing. I suppose everything had been tidied away and washed up by the time the police got on to it.'

'Yes, naturally, but that wasn't for a day or two, you know. If I'd had the faintest idea —'

'No use crying over spilt milk . . . or orange juice for that matter. Was the glass clean or dirty when you were there?'

'I'm afraid I didn't notice.'

'And the jug, could you see how much there was in it?'

'I took no notice of that either.'

'Perhaps you can tell me then whether you think she had been given the overdose before you saw her.'

'I'm almost certain she hadn't had it.'

'You said she seemed better. Couldn't that have been because the Drowse had had a calming effect, the first symptom before she went to sleep?'

'Not possible. I examined her briefly, you know. I'm sure if she'd had anything, even a normal dose, which of course I had strictly forbidden, I should have known it.'

'How long would the stuff take to work?'

'That depends entirely upon the individual. As you know, I was called in at five o'clock the next morning. Dera had been looking in on Dolly at about half-hour intervals all night, I think, but Dolly's breathing had been laboured ever since she came into the nursing-home, so Dera noticed nothing wrong. It was the fact that there was no sound at all the last time she went in that alerted her; she examined the patient, and then called me. And Matron, of course. I can't say, of my own knowledge — that's the phrase you like, isn't it? — whether she had been already dead when Dera first noticed something was wrong, but she was certainly dead by the time I got there.'

'We'll go back to the previous evening then. You saw Dera when you went in, and that was all.'

'No, I'm sorry, I'd forgotten till just this minute. Dera

was back at the desk again when I left Dolly, and Matron was with her.'

'Was that usual?' That was said with carefully suppressed eagerness; it was probably the last thing Vera wanted to hear.

'Like me, she'd make an extra round if circumstances warranted it. She was perfectly well aware of Dolly's condition, of course, I wasn't in the least surprised to see her.'

'No, I can see that. This matter of opportunity though . . . it's an awkward one, isn't it?'

'That, I'm glad to say, is not a thing I need worry about myself.'

'Isn't it, Doctor, isn't it?' He made a gesture that included his two companions. 'We're willing to do all we can, but we can't do a thing without your help, you know.'

'I suppose not,' said Swinburne unwillingly.

'Unless the killing was done on a sudden impulse, possession of the key of the poison cupboard isn't really material.'

'How do you make that out?'

'Because, if it was premeditated, anybody could have provided themselves with the Drowse beforehand. Dera was on duty that night – '

'You're not going to tell me you think she did it, because I won't believe you,' said the doctor roundly.

'No, I'm exonerating her, and on the same grounds that you do . . . purely illogical.' (Though I have to remember that her brother Jackie wasn't above being taken in by a scoundrel.) 'What I was going to ask you was whether anyone could have got to Miss Pritchard's room that night, after your visit – you see, I'm taking your word for that – without Dera seeing them?'

'I left Matron there,' said the doctor doubtfully. 'I suppose that she went in, as that was what she'd come for.'

'Yes, I suppose so too.' He was deliberately avoiding Vera's eye.

'But, you know – you've met her, Maitland! – that's quite unthinkable too.'

'Come now, Doctor,' – Antony was amused, but the sharpness of his tone hid it well enough – 'we'll soon have the whole of Chedcombe exonerated at this rate.'

'Well, if you think –'

'I don't think anything. I'm just trying to find out a few facts. And you haven't told me whether anybody could have got to Miss Pritchard's room without Dera seeing them.'

Swinburne still had a doubtful look, but he spent a little time thinking the question over. 'I don't think anybody could be absolutely sure of not being seen,' he said after a while. 'But it would be perfectly possible, of course, because Dera is on call by all the patients, and might be expected to spend a good time away from her post.'

'One of the nurses, however, could always provide a good excuse if she was seen?'

'Good enough to satisfy Dera, I'm sure, she's a simple soul.'

'But you don't think a member of the general public would have risked it?'

'I certainly don't. But the question doesn't arise really; they couldn't have got into the house.'

'Nurse Mohamad's statement is quite clear on that point,' said Byron, coming suddenly into the conversation. 'She saw nobody that night but Roger and the Matron.'

'And her statement, of course, does not include any information about the other deaths,' said Maitland ruefully. 'Well, we'll have to do what we can with what we've got.'

'Does that mean you're not not going to make any further enquiries?' asked Swinburne bluntly.

'Don't worry, he'll be making them.' Vera's tone expressed no doubt at all. 'Only thing is, we can't talk to the prosecution witnesses. Expect Fred explained that to you.'

Dr Swinburne turned and smiled at her. 'I'm glad of the assurance, of course,' he said, but then he turned back to Maitland again. 'Is she right?' he asked.

86

'Perfectly correct, but don't expect any miracles.' He pushed his chair under the table with a final gesture. 'Before we go, though, there is always the question a lawyer must put to his client in a case like this, concerning a change of plea.'

'I don't know what you mean.'

'He means, pleading Guilty to a mercy killing,' said Byron, also on his feet.

'But there's no question . . . a happy person like Dolly. Apart from the fact it isn't true, nobody would believe it.'

'A jury might.'

'Well, I won't do it!' For a long moment his eyes met Maitland's. 'Is that what you think of me?' Swinburne asked, and for the first time there seemed to be some bitterness in his tone.

Antony shook his head. 'Whatever I think, it isn't that,' he said. 'Well now, Mr Byron will be arranging some interviews for us, and I expect he'll let you know how things go on. But at this stage . . . no promises.'

'May I say, I'm grateful?'

'On the whole, I'd rather you didn't.' Vera, too, was on her feet now and he started towards the door. 'And don't say,' he added, with something that was almost a snarl, 'that you're sure I'll do my best!'

III

By the time they got back to Chedcombe, they all felt that the day had gone on long enough. Frederick Byron promised to do some telephoning from his home, and they arranged a meeting for the first thing the following morning. Vera and Antony went into the George, where they were received with enthusiasm by the elderly waiter (who hadn't been on duty at lunchtime) and led to two chairs near the window of the lounge which, his manner implied, he had been keeping especially for them. It was obvious that Vera's wedding had been a little more than a nine days' wonder in the town where she had lived so long, but Maitland remembered now that the old man had always been one of her staunchest admirers.

They weren't alone in the room, of course, but where they were sitting, well away from the fire, there was no one to overhear them. 'Do we dine in the Bar Mess this evening?' Antony enquired idly, when the waiter had brought their sherry and gone away again.

'Suppose we should,' said Vera, not too enthusiastically. To be in Chedcombe without her own home to retire to obviously seemed to her very strange, and perhaps a little frightening.

'All your old friends,' said Antony enticingly. 'And Wellesley may be there; I'd like to see him.'

'All right then, that's what we'll do.'

'There's one thing that's puzzling me though,' – he had sipped some of his sherry by now, and perhaps it gave him confidence – 'how the Dickens did you know, before I'd answered Swinburne's question, that I was going to go on with the investigation?'

Vera smiled at him. 'Something Geoffrey Horton once told me,' she said. (Horton was a solicitor who had often briefed Maitland in the past, and was also his friend.) 'Said you never snapped at a client with whom you weren't a little in sympathy.'

'I never snapped at the doctor,' said Maitland, horrified.

'You were a little sharp with him once or twice.' Vera's tone was indulgent. 'And you needn't worry about me you know.'

He didn't pretend to misunderstand her. 'Uncle Nick thought –'

'I know quite well what he thought, but he doesn't know Mary Dudley. Every faith in her myself. For that matter,' added Vera, not meeting his eye now, 'every faith in you, not to make a mess of things.'

The compliment was so unexpected that he spluttered a

little over his sherry. 'That's all right then,' he said feebly, when he had recovered himself.

That night in the Bar Mess, Lady Harding was greeted with great delight by her former brothers-in-law. She was less shy now than this demonstration would at one time have made her, and Antony wished his uncle could have been there, he thought he would have been proud of her.

But when they parted for the night, and in spite of the lateness of the hour he telephoned home, he revised his opinion a little. Sir Nicholas, according to Jenny, was in one of his more captious moods, missing his wife, and maintaining stoutly that her absence was all his nephew's fault.

# I

When he communicated this to Vera the next morning at breakfast she was thoughtful for a while, and when Antony taxed her with absentmindedness she admitted that she now felt it had been a mistake to involve herself in the initial investigation. 'Not trying to back out of the trial,' she assured him, 'but in the meantime you'll get on just as well without me . . . perhaps better. And if Nicholas is missing me –'

Maitland grinned at her. 'I expect that means you're missing him too,' he said reflectively. And then, with intent to provoke, 'But are you sure you can trust me alone with this delicate matter?'

'Should have done so from the beginning,' said Vera flatly.

That deserved some comment. 'When the trial comes on, you shall cross-examine Miss Dudley yourself,' Antony offered. It was the utmost he could think of in the way of concessions, and something in Vera's gruff 'Thank you' told him that she appreciated it as such.

However, it was a morning of surprises. Before they had finished their coffee Vera was called to the phone, and came back nearly ten minutes later with a slightly heightened colour and the assertion, 'He wants to talk to you, too.'

That could only mean Uncle Nick. Antony went out to the dark booth in the hall, wondering vaguely what was up. 'I hear you thought better of having Vera with you,' said Sir Nicholas's voice accusingly, almost before he had had time to say Hello.

'Nothing of the kind. Didn't she explain to you that it was her own idea?'

'She said so, certainly. Tactful,' said Sir Nicholas, with something of his wife's manner.

'Well, don't you think it's a good idea for her to come home?'

'No, I do not. She tells me you've decided that your client is innocent.'

'I wouldn't go quite so far as that,' said Antony cautiously.

'How far would you go then?'

'I think some further investigation is justified, and I should like to conduct it myself. Vera knows I value her advice, but . . . she wants to be with you, Uncle Nick.' He added that last bit of information in a rush, because it was uncommonly difficult to say.

'No reason why she shouldn't be,' Sir Nicholas informed him. 'I shall catch the afternoon train.'

'You mean . . . come to Chedcombe?'

'I thought I had made myself sufficiently clear.'

'But I know you said you would be in court – '

'My client has pneumonia; it is a sickly season,' said Sir Nicholas, with more satisfaction than the statement seemed to warrant. 'And even Mallory agrees with me that there's no reason I shouldn't take a few days off.'

'But '

'Are you hiding something from me, Antony?'

'Nothing at all. What could I be hiding?' he asked reasonably.

'You seem strangely reluctant to have me join you.'

'Well, Uncle Nick, you've always said if I came out of town during an assize I couldn't take Jenny with me. It seems to me that what's sauce for the gander – ' That had nothing to do with his reason for not wanting Sir Nicholas to come to Chedcombe, as he knew well enough; the real reason lay somewhere in his sub-conscious, and for the moment it eluded him.

'I don't altogether appreciate the comparison between your aunt and a goose,' said Sir Nicholas austerely. 'But if it'll make you feel any better we will remove ourselves to the other hostelry, the Angel I believe it's called, across the square. Perhaps you'll be kind enough to make the arrangements.'

Antony knew when he was beaten. 'I'll make the booking for you,' he said, 'and see that Vera meets the afternoon train.'

'Thank you. You might also make a booking for three for dinner tonight. We shall expect you,' said Sir Nicholas, and rang off without waiting for his nephew's reply.

Back in the dining-room, Maitland found that Vera had ordered fresh coffee. 'Did you succeed in dissuading him?' she asked as he seated himself.

'No, I didn't. How did you know I was going to try?'

'Thought you might, that's all.'

'Well, if you can tell me why I shouldn't want him to come — ' He waited a moment, but when Vera did not respond to that appeal he went on, 'You're to move to the Angel. I've been instructed to make the booking. And to join you there for dinner tonight. I promised you'd meet the afternoon train, which wasn't a very good idea, because I think our interviews will take most of the day.'

'Been thinking about that,' Vera told him. 'Too many people, subject less likely to talk. Do better on your own, I shouldn't wonder.'

'Well, of the two of you I'd rather dispense with Frederick Byron,' said Maitland thoughtfully. 'But I don't think he'd take kindly to that suggestion, do you?'

'Knowing Fred . . . no, I don't. He's a good sort of man, you know, but conventional. Think you'd do better without me though,' Vera repeated. 'I'll take my time packing up and moving across to the Angel, and then take a walk if it stops raining. Glad to see something of the town again.'

'We could meet for lunch.'

'Don't tie yourself down. Let's just say I'll be lunching here at one o'clock, join me if you can.'

So Maitland was alone when he entered Frederick

Byron's office. By whatever magic the solicitor had used, he had managed by some means to arrange for the bulk of the interviews Antony had asked for to be held there. 'Though they were none of them particularly co-operative,' he admitted. 'The Reynoldses, and the Newboulds, and Ian Stewart, and Bill Sanders will all come in this afternoon. That leaves us with this morning free.'

'And just as well really; we can discuss the statements of some of the prosecution witnesses.'

'Vera isn't with you?'

'No, she decided these particular interviews would be better with two people present than with three.'

'Is she going back to London then for the time being?'

'No, my uncle is coming down here for a few days.' If Byron thought it was an odd time of year to be taking a holiday, he made no comment. 'What about Nurse Booth?'

'She seems to prefer to see you at the residence. I hope you won't find that too inconvenient.'

'On the contrary, it will fill in some time later this morning. And I thought after we've had our talk that I ought to see Mr Williamson too, the manager of the hotel, just in case he can tell us anything.'

'It certainly can't do any harm,' Byron agreed, without any enthusiasm. He spread a pile of documents into a sort of fan on the desk in front of him and looked at them with a dissatisfied air. 'Would you like some coffee before we start?' he asked.

'No coffee, thank you. I drank more than my ration at breakfast.'

'Perhaps later,' said Byron vaguely. And then, still with that rather distracted air, 'Shall we start with the medical evidence?'

'I don't see much point in it. There's no question – is there? – as to how Dolly Pritchard died.'

'No question at all.'

'I'll do my homework on it of course before the trial, just in case anything crops up. But as there's no disputing how the old lady died . . . as I say, I think we can use our time better on other things.'

'Roger's treatment of the patient may be questioned,' Byron warned him.

'I doubt it. With enough Drowse in her to kill a horse, or so I gather, there'd be no point in him fluffing the other medication. However, I promise I'll familiarise myself with all that before the trial.'

'Where do you want to begin then?' asked Byron, resigned to leaving the medical details alone, but taking a certain satisfaction nevertheless in sending the ball into the other man's court.

'Who is the investigating officer?'

'Detective Inspector Camden.'

'Good Lord, hasn't he been promoted yet?'

'That doesn't come so quickly in places like this, you know. Though I dare say if he'd been willing to leave Chedcombe things might have been different.'

'I remember him as a very thorough man,' said Maitland reminiscently.

'Yes, you've had several encounters with him, haven't you? I imagine he remembers you too. Your previous visits to Chedcombe,' said Byron, with that hint of dryness in his voice, 'have been – shall we say? – enlivening.'

'You may say what you like, but personally I'd rather forget all about them,' Antony told him. 'However, Inspector Camden and his minions came into the case in response to Miss Veronica Pritchard's complaints. Once the results of the *post mortem* were known, he doesn't seem to have had much difficulty in making up his mind about the guilty party.'

'You'll have gathered that Roger Swinburne is a friend of mine,' said Frederick Byron slowly. 'All the same, in view of the evidence, I don't see what else Camden could have done.'

'After two days or so, in a place as well cared for as the

nursing-home, there could have been nothing left in the way of material clues.'

'But both the main points against him are very strong,' Byron pointed out. 'Motive . . . well, he was a little non-committal when you talked to him about his financial position, but there's more that could be brought out in court.'

'Yes, I rather wondered about that.'

'I don't really think you could expect Roger to be any more open about it. It's Sylvia, you see, his wife.'

'What about Sylvia?'

'She's a fine person in many ways.' Byron sounded fairly uncomfortable now. 'But she *is* extravagant, I have to admit that.'

'And that fact, of course, is well known in the town.' Maitland sounded depressed. 'Who have the police unearthed to provide that bit of evidence?'

'A couple of the local tradesmen, heavy bills run up, not paid too promptly. In particular the boutique' – he grimaced a little over the word – 'where she bought most of her clothes.'

'Did she confide in her husband?'

'That's something I haven't asked him. I imagine she wouldn't do so until it was forced upon her. But I'm probably giving you the wrong impression, Maitland; they're a very affectionate couple. Well suited to each other.'

'I'm glad to hear it.' Antony's tone, in turn, was a little dry. 'That ties up the motive nicely, and we can't deny opportunity. The prosecution have Matron's evidence, and Dera's for that.'

'Yes, that's really the main part of their case, though there's also the fact – which it may take cross-examination to bring out – that Roger was on rather more familiar terms with Miss Pritchard than with any of the other patients. Even than with the three chronic cases whom he saw every day, month in and month out.'

'He denied that.'

'I expect he quite genuinely thinks of himself as impartial.'

'That may be so. In any case,' said Maitland more cheerfully, 'it could be accounted for – couldn't it? – by Dolly Pritchard's very outgoing temperament.'

'As long as you can make the jury understand that,' said Byron in a dejected way.

'I shall do my best. Let's see, you said Nurse Hardaker was to be a witness for the prosecution too, didn't you? I suppose her evidence is more of the same . . . the close relationship between the doctor and this particular patient.'

'I'm afraid there's rather more to it than that.' Since their talk began the solicitor had been fiddling with his paper-knife; now he was stabbing at his blotting pad with it in a nervous way. 'This is something I should have told you yesterday when you arrived, Mr Maitland, only I was dreading the interview in the prison, and didn't want the matter brought up.'

'If it's something important it will have to be brought up sooner or later. I suppose you mean you think our client may not have a good explanation.'

'Not that exactly,' said Byron. He seemed in some doubt as to how to proceed. 'But Nurse Hardaker says she overheard Roger talking to old Miss Pritchard one day. Her expression was that he was "getting round her" . . . talking about the cost of living, the expense of running a practice, the necessity for a professional man to keep up appearances.'

'You're quite right, that's something I should have been told about.' Maitland's tone was oddly unemphatic. 'Was there any more?'

'Only that another day she was going into the room as he was leaving. She saw him pat Miss Pritchard's hand and say, "We understand each other, don't we, Dolly?" and then he broke off because he saw her in the doorway.'

'On my understanding, Miss Pritchard was only in the nursing-home two days before she died.'

'Two full days. Both those conversations took place on his morning visit, one the first day, one the second.'

'I should have asked you this before. When was the will made?'

'About a month before Dolly died.'

'Then these conversations could only be interpreted as attempts to prevent her from changing her mind. But even so — ' Maitland was on his feet. He went over to the fire, which was burning a little sulkily, and stood looking down at it. 'You're too embarrassed to mention his wife's extravagance to him,' he said. 'Too embarrassed to ask for an explanation of this very damning bit of evidence. I think this is a case where our client may be the loser by having a friend to act for him.'

'Yes, I realise that, only too well. But I could hardly retire from the case without having people think I believed Roger guilty. I'm sorry to have made things more difficult, but I'm telling you now.'

'Are you sure these are the only pieces of information you've withheld?'

'Yes, quite sure. And if you will forgive my saying so, Mr Maitland,' said Byron a little stiffly, 'that remark was quite uncalled for.'

Antony turned then and smiled at him. 'If you think for a minute you'll see it wasn't uncalled for at all,' he said. 'But there's no use going over and over it, if you're sure I've got all the facts now. The thing is, when can we see Swinburne again? Or would you rather I went to the prison alone?'

'If you're going up to Restawhile this morning,' said Byron, 'the only chance I can see is late this afternoon. I ought to accompany you — '

'Don't worry about that. My proceedings as a whole are sufficiently unorthodox to make that immaterial. So ring up the prison now, there's a good chap, and then we can phone Mr Williamson at the hotel and find out if he can see us.'

# II

Mr Williamson, the manager of the Restawhile Hotel, was a tall, thin, grey man, with a leisurely air that might or might not be illusory. Frederick Byron he knew already, but he greeted Maitland's introduction to him rather too eagerly for Antony's taste. He felt the words 'I've heard of you, Mr Maitland' hovering in the air, and hastened into speech before they could be uttered.

'It's good of you to see us, Mr Williamson.'

This trite remark was greeted with more respect than it deserved; Williamson seemed to be regarding it from all angles before he attempted to reply. Then he said, 'I have to admit, I'm interested, I think everybody is in these legal affairs. But I can't for the life of me see how I can be of help to you.'

'We have to try everything,' Antony told him. 'Have you been running this place long?'

'For the past ten years or so.'

'Then you must know a good deal about the guests. But before we go into that, tell me something . . . who gave the hotel its name?'

'Restawhile?' He smiled, as Antony had hoped he would. 'It's pretty frightful, isn't it? I don't know who was responsible in the first place, but the hotel has been open since just after the war, and by the time I took over it was much too late to make any change.'

'Then we must get back to more serious matters.' He saw Byron frowning over the exchange, and wished again that he could have conducted these interviews alone. 'I'm afraid that what I'm going to ask you may seem to you to be an impertinence, Mr Williamson. But I'm not asking for any details of the hotel's affairs, or those of any of the guests. There are things of general knowledge, however, that you may feel able to tell me. General knowledge in Chedcombe, I mean, but that are unknown to me as a stranger here.'

'I don't understand you, I'm afraid.' Williamson was polite but bewildered.

'I've been hearing something from Mr Byron here about your late guest, Miss Dolly Pritchard, her financial affairs, her will.'

'Then I don't see what you can want from me.'

'You will know that Matron — Miss Dudley — has been very worried by talk in the town about three deaths that occurred in the nursing-home, before Miss Pritchard went there. You must know something about the three old people concerned, their friends and relations . . . or if you prefer to put it another way, their heirs, executors and assigns.'

'But I understood — it's only Miss Pritchard's death, surely, that concerns you?'

'In the interests of my client,' Antony told him, 'I'm making the other three deaths my concern as well. I could get the details of Mrs Reynolds' estate quite easily, I expect, as she died six months ago. But I don't suppose the others have been admitted to probate yet.'

'But why should you want to know?'

'Because, now that it is certain that Miss Pritchard didn't die naturally, I am as sceptical as Chedcombe is about the cause of the earlier deaths.'

'And you want to know . . . I don't think I can help you, Mr Maitland.'

'I'm not asking you to reveal any confidences, only to tell me what is probably quite generally talked of in the hotel.'

There was no lightness in Williamson's manner now. Again he weighed the question carefully. 'Ask your questions,' he said at last, 'and then we'll see.'

'Well, let's take the three cases in turn. For one thing, I understand the hotel isn't exactly inexpensive.'

That brought another smile from Williamson. 'I think

you might say that,' he agreed. 'But in all fairness I have to add that we do give value for money.'

'I'm sure you do, but that isn't the point. Mrs Reynolds, now. Did she pay her own way?'

'Certainly she did.'

'She had no children of her own?'

'No, she was rather a lonely old lady really. Full of life, and enjoyed talking to her friends in the hotel. But, of course, nothing much happens there, so visitors from outside are always welcome. And I must say her nephew and his wife, who wasn't really a relation at all, were very assiduous in coming to see her.'

'Vernon and Dorothy Reynolds?'

'That's right.'

'Do you think she enjoyed their visits?'

'That's a funny question. I always assumed she did.'

'And after she died? Was he her heir?'

'Now, that I can tell you, because there was some talk about it among the guests. I think the size of the estate surprised everybody, and, apart from some minor bequests to charities and to her church, everything went to Vernon Reynolds.'

'So we come to Mrs Henley.'

'I must say,' said Williamson, 'if you're thinking she was murdered you must add me to the list of suspects.' (Thank Heaven the man had a sense of humour.) 'She was definitely one of my trials, not an easy person to get on with, and sometimes even a cause of dissension among the other guests.' He seemed to be getting into his swing now, to have forgotten his earlier misgivings. 'I don't think she even liked her daughter very much – that's Mrs Francis Newbould. And Betty Newbould didn't visit her very often; I don't really think she can be blamed for that.'

'They both – Mr and Mrs Newbould – went to see her while she was in the nursing-home, but the doctor had said "No visitors". Were there any other relations?'

'Not that I know of. Anyway, it doesn't really concern

us, because I expect your next question is going to be about the will, isn't it?'

'It will be a bit of luck for me if you know about that too.'

'Well, as you said, it's too early for probate yet. But in this case that doesn't apply. Mr Crayshaw told me that she had been living on an annuity, so there was nothing to leave.'

'Is Mr Crayshaw another of your guests?'

'Yes, he is. The one there is in every place like this, who knows everything.'

'Did he tell you about Mr Stewart's will too?'

'There was never any secret about that. Mr Stewart had just the one son, Ian, and he always said everything was going to him. I imagine – and here I'm guessing, Mr Maitland – that he had plenty to leave. I'm judging from the way he lived, the way he spent money freely.'

'Do you know Ian Stewart?'

'Fairly well, he was a frequent visitor. Not my type, but old Donald seemed fond of him. We miss him quite a bit – the old man, I mean – he was a friendly soul.'

'I'm grateful for your help, Mr Williamson.' (Probably more grateful than you will ever know.) 'That brings me to the only question you may feel I have a right to ask you: what can you tell me about Miss Pritchard?'

'Oh, Dolly!' He smiled again, and his voice was warm with amusement. 'She was really our star turn, you know, everybody's friend. And you don't need to ask me about her will, because that's common knowledge now, and you of all people must know all about it.'

Maitland glanced at his instructing solicitor before he answered. 'Unfortunately, we do know all about it,' he agreed. 'All the same, I should like to know about this niece of hers . . . I should say great-niece, I understand.'

'I know nothing that the whole town couldn't tell you. Very respectable young woman I believe, a school teacher, I think her subject is mathematics. She always came to tea at Restawhile on Sundays, and the last three or four weeks she brought her new fiancé with her.'

Maitland was consulting one of his battered envelopes. 'Bill Sanders,' he said triumphantly after a moment.

'That's right, a nice young fellow he seemed. One of the professions –'

'An architect,' Maitland supplied.

'He called her Ronnie, which tickled Dolly no end, though she must have heard other people do it before. She is perhaps a little bit prim, you know . . . the younger Miss Pritchard, I mean.'

'I got the impression that she was a little older than Mr Sanders.'

'That would be my impression, too, but of course I don't really know.'

'Did you like her?' asked Maitland with one of his attacks of bluntness.

For the first time Williamson showed some embarrassment. 'I really didn't know her well enough to say,' he answered after a moment. Which was really as revealing as any reply he could have made.

'Has she any money of her own?'

'That's something quite outside my knowledge.'

'Doesn't even Mr Crayshaw know?' asked Maitland, smiling.

'The subject has never come up. But if you want my impression, it's that she had nothing beyond her salary.'

'Do you think she expected to inherit?'

'You do ask the most damnable questions, Mr Maitland. It's something I obviously can't answer. It may never have crossed her mind, but as Dolly's only relative I should think she must have had expectations, wouldn't you?'

'I should think so too, and she wouldn't be human if it hadn't occurred to her. Now there's just one more thing, Mr Williamson. I believe Doctor Swinburne was in regular attendance on Dolly Pritchard.'

'Yes, he saw her about two or three times a week. And he

had warned me about her heart condition. It wasn't easy to stop her exerting herself, but one of the maids was always told off to keep an eye on her. That was about the best we could do.'

'And a very good best I'm sure it was. Were you ever present when he examined her?'

'No, of course not. But sometimes it was just a matter of him having a word or two with her in the lounge. Then I might be in the room, you know, though not listening to what they had to say.'

'You can tell me at least, did you ever observe any extraordinary intimacy in their manner towards each other?'

'Doctor Swinburne has a very friendly, easy manner. I should say he treated her no differently from any of the other guests.'

Antony glanced at Frederick Byron. 'Have I missed anything?' he asked.

'Nothing that I can think of,' said Byron, but he shook his head as he spoke as though he were in some little doubt.

'Then I'll thank you again for your courtesy.' Maitland came to his feet. 'And in case you have second thoughts about your wisdom in answering my questions, let me add that we're not out to make trouble.'

'But you'd like to prove some connection between the three earlier deaths and Dolly Pritchard's,' said Williamson shrewdly.

'What do you think about it . . . honestly?'

'The hotel has been rife with rumours, you know, ever since Mrs Henley died. But even after Mr Stewart's death I could never bring myself to believe that there was anything in it. And when Dolly Pritchard died, it wasn't unexpected. And now it's been proved . . . but I like Doctor Swinburne, I'd like you to prove his innocence. Though it does strike me that in doing so you may be letting us in for an even bigger scandal.'

'If it's the truth –'

'Yes, of course, that's the most important thing.'

'What do your guests say now?'

'They're pretty well evenly divided in their opinions. Half say Doctor Swinburne couldn't possibly . . . the others aren't so sure.'

'And the omniscient Mr Crayshaw?'

'He's a partisan of the doctor's.'

'In that case . . . look here, Mr Williamson, we may be calling you for the defence.'

'How on earth can I help?'

'By saying, very simply, just what you told us just now. That Doctor Swinburne's manner was no different with Miss Pritchard than with any of your other guests, and that he was concerned enough about her condition to confide in you about it.'

'I see. That sounds straightforward enough.' They were moving towards the door as they spoke. 'Of course, I'll be pleased to do anything I can.'

Frederick Byron was looking thoughtful as they went out into the street. 'Do you really think that will help?' he asked.

'At least, it can't do any harm. And, of course, there's Mr Crayshaw, who knows everything. Do you think we ought to see him?'

'Gossip,' said Byron bitterly.

'Oh, I don't know. I think we should fight the town with its own weapons, but we can always come back to him later if nothing else turns up. Meanwhile, I wonder if Nurse Booth will be waiting for us.'

## III

Shirley Booth turned out to be a slight, sharp-faced girl with thin arms, who looked no more capable than Dera Mohamad did of handling a heavy patient. She was waiting in the big drawing-room of the nurses' residence when they arrived there; whether this was an instance of Frederick Byron's efficiency or of Matron's, Antony couldn't make up his mind. 'I'm sure I don't know what you want to talk to me for,' she said rather disagreeably, almost before the introductions were made.

'You understand the position, I'm sure Mr Byron must have explained it to you,' said Maitland, resisting well enough the temptation to reply in kind. 'There are a few questions we should like to ask you.'

'You've no right. I said I would see you because Matron asked me to, but I don't have to answer your questions.'

'Do you dislike Doctor Swinburne so very much?'

'I don't dislike him at all. At least, not particularly. He's a man, he can look after himself.'

'Then I think I shall have to ask Mr Byron to explain the legal position to you. It's perfectly true that you don't have to answer our questions now, but you could be *sub poena*'d as a witness for the defence, and if you didn't answer in court you'd stand in contempt.'

She thought about that for a moment. 'Is that right?' she said eventually, turning to the solicitor.

'A very precise statement of the facts,' Byron confirmed.

'Well, all right then. But if you're trying to drag in the other three deaths,' she added shrewishly, 'there's nothing doing. You couldn't do that in court.'

Privately – in spite of the rather glib statements he had been making about basing the defence on showing method – Maitland thought she was only too right about that. 'It would be a matter for the judge to decide,' he said. 'However, if you prefer it, we can confine ourselves to Miss Dolly Pritchard's death.'

'I don't know anything about that. I wasn't on night duty.'

'You had been on duty though, during the day?'

'Yes, I was on from two o'clock until ten at night. There was too much to do, she was a nuisance, Miss Pritchard was, always wanting something.'

'You were there then when Doctor Swinburne made his first call?'

'Yes, I was, but if you're asking me to tell you what time it was I can't do that, I was far too busy to notice.'

'Did you at any time observe anything special in the doctor's relationship with Miss Pritchard?'

'No, I didn't. Why should I? He fancies himself about having a good bedside manner, but there's nothing in that.'

'I see. I wonder, Nurse, can you tell me, has Nurse Hardaker any particular grievance against Doctor Swinburne?'

'Her? No, I wouldn't say that. She gets on with everybody,' said Nurse Booth contemptuously. She made it sound as though this was in some way an undesirable trait.

'What can you tell me about Miss Dolly Pritchard?'

'Nothing much. She was in our side more than most, and always a nuisance.'

'By "our side" you mean in the nursing-home?'

'What else would I mean?'

After all, probably Mr Williamson had told him as much as could usefully be known about Miss Pritchard's affairs. Why persist in face of this girl's hostility? They couldn't call her; a nice showing she would make in court!

Maitland turned away and walked across to the window, and stood for a moment looking out. Then he turned on her suddenly. 'Did *you* start the original rumours that all the deaths in the nursing-home weren't natural?' he asked.

He was pretty sure if the question hadn't been sprung on her like that she would have denied it. As it was, her eyes fell before his and she said sulkily, 'I may have said something to Marian, something about it being a little funny. But there's no need to start rumours in Chedcombe, they spring up by themselves.'

'Yes, I have to agree with you there,' he said a little ruefully. 'Besides the nurse on night duty —'

'Dera Mohamad, that night,' she said spitefully.

' — would it be difficult for any unauthorised person to get into the nursing-home at night?'

'You'd have to have a key.' She was certain enough about that.

'The doctor has a key, I suppose, and the nurses?'

'All the nurses. And Matron,' she added.

'Yes, I was taking that for granted. And any of the staff, I suppose, if they were seen, even if it wasn't their time on duty, could produce some story to explain their presence?'

'I dare say that's true,' she admitted grudgingly. And then, with more confidence, 'For instance, Matron's often over there at night. She was there the night Mrs Henley died.'

'Are you sure about that?'

'Of course I'm sure. I saw her from the window, crossing the road, and she was in uniform.'

'What time was this?'

'I don't remember, exactly. Later than her usual rounds, anyway. But what I'm saying is, nobody would ask her to explain and nobody would be surprised, least of all that little ninny, Dera.'

'So it isn't at all impossible that the three deaths that started all the talk . . . come, Nurse Booth, it was your idea in the first place.'

'I suppose it isn't impossible, but I've changed my mind now,' she said firmly. 'Anyway, I'm not answering questions about them, I told you that in the beginning.'

'So you did.' He was still standing with his back to the window, but now he came across the room again. 'In that case, Nurse, it only remains to thank you for your help,' he said formally. And this time he did not ask Frederick Byron whether anything had been forgotten.


# IV

Byron had a luncheon engagement of his own, but promised to be available again by two o'clock. Antony went back to the George, and thought that after the company of the abrasive Nurse Booth he could do with a drink even before Vera joined him. In the event, however, that had to be delayed. No sooner had he got to his room than the telephone rang. And the receptionist (faintly apologetic, so that Antony was reminded of Hill, in chambers) announced briefly, 'Detective Inspector Camden would like to see you, Mr Maitland.'

There was only one answer to that. If they met in the lounge, half of Chedcombe would know within the hour. 'Ask him to come up to my room,' said Antony with as good grace as he could manage. Though, like his other encounters in the town, it wasn't one he was looking forward to.

As usual, his first thought, when the detective came in, was that he was rather short for a policeman. Camden was a dark man, extremely impassive, whose face looked as if it had been inexpertly carved out of a piece of wood. He said, 'So we meet again, Mr Maitland,' by way of greeting, which wasn't exactly encouraging. But then his memories of their previous dealings were probably as unpleasant as Antony's own.

If you wanted bluntness, Maitland was only too glad to oblige. 'I said I'd see you, Inspector, but I'm not at all sure that we aren't out of order in talking together. You're the investigating officer in the Pritchard case, aren't you? And you must know that Doctor Swinburne is my client.'

'I don't really need reminding of the custom in these cases,' said Camden coldly. 'As it happens, it isn't about the Pritchard case that I wish to speak to you. Well, not exactly,' he added, with unwilling honesty.

'What else, exactly, is there for us to talk about?'

'You're going beyond your brief,' said Camden, abandoning finesse.

Antony laughed. Both men were still standing, but now he waved the inspector to the armchair near the window, and perched himself on the stool by the dressing-table. 'And if I am,' he said lightly, 'I don't honestly see what it has to do with you.'

'Perhaps nothing, in the ordinary way.' Camden seemed to be making a genuine effort to explain himself. 'But what goes on in this town *is* my affair. Chedcombe is a funny place – '

'Strike a spark and the tinder is dry,' agreed Maitland sympathetically. 'All the same, I can't let your troubles, or possible troubles, interfere with my handling of a case.'

'Doctor Swinburne is accused of killing his patient, Dolly Pritchard, and for a very good reason. You're trying to drag in three other deaths, all completely motiveless.'

'All without motives so far as the doctor is concerned,' Antony corrected him. 'And you'll agree, if I could show method – '

'That's something you can't possibly do.'

'There might be ways. If you were to talk to the coroner now – '

'Mr Maitland!' Camden sounded shocked. 'You know as well as I do there's no excuse for one exhumation, let alone three.'

'I was afraid you'd say that,' said Antony sadly. Then he brightened. 'But there's no saying how the judge may look at it, you know.'

'He won't take that up, any more than the coroner will.'

'I was thinking more of what might be allowed in the way of cross-examination,' said Antony. 'But you promised not to discuss the Pritchard case, Inspector, and if that's not what we're doing I don't know what it is.'

'Very well, Mr Maitland, very well.' For such an impassive man, Camden could sound quite threatening. He began to move towards the door, saying over his shoulder, 'Don't blame me if there's trouble, though.'

'I won't. But, wait a bit, Inspector, there's one thing I should very much like to know.' Camden stopped with his hand on the door knob. 'Which of my prospective witnesses has complained to you?'

'I didn't need any complaint,' said Camden. 'This is my town, and I don't like interference.'

'All the same, something prompted you to come to me.' He paused, and saw with satisfaction that the inspector had reddened a little. 'Well, if you won't tell me you won't,' he said, resigned. 'I shall have to play a guessing game, that's all.'

## V

'Doesn't want any more trouble,' said Vera in her plain-spoken way, when he met her ten minutes later in the lounge. 'Don't know that I blame him, really, difficult to deal with.'

'But surely, my dear Vera, with you here to keep me on the right lines . . . *and* Uncle Nick,' he added, hoping for a rise.

'Laughing at me,' said Vera, without rancour.

'I wouldn't dare. Seriously though, I think my guess was right, someone has been talking to him. And, if so, it means that some one of the people Byron phoned for appointments dislikes the prospect of my questions.'

'May be right,' said Vera, humouring him. She paused while the waiter brought her sherry, and a large Black Label for Maitland. 'Want to know what I think?' she said, when the man had gone. 'Doesn't matter either way. So you may as well tell me what you've been up to this morning.'

## VI

Maitland walked across to Frederick Byron's office at about ten minutes to two, and found the solicitor struggling with a fire that had grown sulky again. Probably the chimney needed sweeping. 'There's one thing that's been puzzling me,' he said, watching the other man's efforts and thinking he could have done better himself. 'How in Heaven's name did you get all these people to agree to see us?'

Byron put down the poker, straightened himself, and smiled. 'You mean, why didn't they stand on their rights as Nurse Booth did? It was quite easy really.'

'Then I wish you'd tell me how it was done.'

'It was merely a matter of suggesting that a refusal might give rise to some speculation.'

'Heaven and Earth! Now if I were to do that . . . what it is to be respectable,' said Maitland enviously.

'It's partly that,' said Byron, giving the remark more consideration than it deserved, 'and partly the small-town fear of gossip. Anyway, they're coming. I allowed half an hour for each interview, an hour for you to get out to the prison – a car has been laid on – and arranged for you to see Roger at five o'clock.'

'That sounds an excellent programme.' The telephone rang sharply as he spoke, and he added with a grin, 'And there, if I mistake not, is our client now.'

It was certainly the first couple they wished to interview, Vernon and Dorothy Reynolds. They were a comfortable-looking couple, much of a height, and both in the vicinity of sixty. About them there was the odd likeness that sometimes comes to couples who have been married for a very long time. Both had curly grey hair, round, rather fresh complexioned faces, and blue eyes with a somehow guileless look. They accepted Fred Byron's introductions without comment, except that each of them in turn nodded at Maitland in quite a friendly way. Then they went quite docilely to the chairs the solicitor indicated in front of his desk, leaving Antony to his great delight free to remain on his feet, with the additional advantage of being able to walk about the room should the mood so take him.

'I have to thank you,' said Byron, seeing that his colleague seemed in no hurry to speak, 'for being good enough to give us some of your time. I'm afraid it may not have been very convenient for you, Mr Reynolds.'

'As far as that goes,' said Reynolds, 'I've no complaint to make. The shops pretty well run themselves by now, leaving me free when I want to be. But I have to admit to being puzzled – '

'We both are,' put in Mrs Reynolds.

' – as to why you should want to see us,' her husband concluded.

'It's all a matter of this gossip that's been going around about your aunt's death,' Byron told them. 'It may not seem to be strictly relevant to our client's affairs, but I think you'll agree we have to look into it.'

They made no reply to that, but again each nodded in turn. Maitland decided it was time he took a hand.

'You'll have to forgive some of my questions,' he said, smiling at Mrs Reynolds, whom he thought might be the more susceptible of the two, 'but, you see, I'm a stranger in Chedcombe, so I have to start at the beginning.'

'Not quite a stranger,' Reynolds corrected him, but not in a contentious way. 'You managed to get yourself into the papers on your previous visits.'

'So I did.' That was said lightly, though he didn't like the reminder. 'However, there are more people who know Tom Fool than Tom Fool knows. And I should be more than grateful if you would tell me a little about your aunt, and about yourselves too.'

'Aunt Anne – Tannie, she was always called – was a very lively old lady. Even when we were younger – I think this is right, don't you, my dear? – we found a little difficulty in keeping pace with her. Even when she decided her own house was too much for her, and went to the hotel, she was still full of projects.'

'Good works?' said Antony, puzzled.

'That wasn't exactly what I meant. She was inclined to interfere in other people's lives, with the best of intentions I'm sure, but there may have been some people who resented it.'

'I see. That's something new to me, and very interesting.' He smiled at the silent Mrs Reynolds again (no harm in buttering her up a little) and said in an amused tone, 'But

I imagine you were more than a match for her, if she tried anything like that with you.'

'There was no question . . . Vernon was just telling you her way with other people. And though she told us, rather too often, that all her old friends were dead, she certainly made many new ones at the hotel. So we used to visit her about once a month, and can't really say we were closely in touch with her before she died.'

'But you did see her in the nursing-home?'

'Oh, yes, several times; she was there a whole week, perhaps a little longer.'

'Were you surprised about what happened?'

'Not really.' Dorothy Reynolds had quite taken over the conversation now. 'An old lady, a broken hip, I've heard of so many cases.'

'Yes, I can see that.'

'Is that all?' she asked hopefully.

'You remember, I was hoping to hear something of you and your husband.'

'Oh, we're very ordinary people. Vernon is more or less retired, though he still keeps an eye on things at the shops.'

'You mentioned that before.' He turned back to her husband. 'What sort of shops?' he asked.

'Furniture,' said Vernon Reynolds briefly. 'One here, and one in Northdean. As for my wife,' – he turned and smiled at her – 'there's never been any reason for her to go out to work.'

'And less than ever now,' said Maitland, rather as though he was speaking to himself.

Dorothy Reynolds bridled – that was the only word for it, though it occurred to him that he had never seen anyone do it before. 'If you mean that Tannie left us her money,' she said, 'I can assure you, we didn't need it.'

'Hush, Dorothy.' (That sounded odd, too, to Maitland's ear.) 'I can quite understand how these questions have arisen, only I do assure you, as my wife says, we really had no need of the money.'

'I'm sure you didn't,' said Antony with a sincerity that was a little too obvious. 'It's good of you,' he added, looking from one to the other of them, 'to take my questions in such good part. As a matter of fact there are only two remaining.'

'What are those?'

'Are you personally acquainted with any of the nurses at the Restawhile Nursing-Home? Or with Miss Dudley, the Matron?'

That brought the first hint of hesitation, they exchanged doubtful glances. 'As for the nurses,' said Vernon after a moment, 'we saw several, of course, but they all look alike in uniform. And Matron we met when we talked to her about Tannie's condition. In fact, it was she who warned us –'

'Warned you?' asked Maitland when the other man did not seem about to continue. 'What did she warn you about?'

'That perhaps her condition was not as stable as it seemed. That was why neither of us was too surprised when – when it happened.'

'When your aunt died?' But the answer to that was obvious; they neither of them attempted to give it.

'She wasn't my aunt,' said Dorothy Reynolds with the first hint of shrewishness that he had noticed in her.

'No, I understand that.' He had been standing at the corner of the desk at Byron's left; now he took a turn towards the door and back, the only area free of furniture. 'I wonder why you should trouble to mention it just at the moment, though.'

'Because it was a thing of which she was only too fond of reminding me.' The smiling mask was back in place again. 'But there, you know as well as I do, Mr Maitland, old people do have their fancies.'

'Would you consider – as next-of-kin you're the one who must answer this, Mr Reynolds – would you consider backing up an application for an exhumation order?'

In spite of what he said, it was again Dorothy Reynolds

who answered. 'Dig Tannie up?' she enquired indignantly. 'We wouldn't dream of allowing anything so degrading.'

# VII

'Well, one thing is clear,' said Maitland, when the visitors had gone about ten minutes later, 'they never saw Dera Mohamad, or they couldn't have said all the nurses look alike.'

'As she seems to be perpetually on night duty, it wasn't likely they would encounter her,' Byron retorted. 'I must say I wasn't aware you were going to sail quite so close to the wind,' he added reflectively, but without censure in his tone. 'They took it well, though, didn't they?'

'Too well,' said Maitland in a sombre tone. He left his place by the desk and walked over to the fire. It was behaving better now, he kicked it into a blaze. 'I've known you for more than seven years, so that's all right, isn't it?' he asked, looking down at the flames.

Byron ignored that. 'How do you mean, too well?' he asked. 'I thought that, under the circumstances, they behaved remarkably well.'

'Oh, so did I. That's all I meant really. Why should they put up with so much impertinence, from me or anybody else?'

'Because they are a naturally obliging couple,' said Byron, a little severely. 'I don't see what there is to complain of in that.'

'Nothing at all. Look here, Mr Byron, what do *you* know about Vernon Reynolds?'

'I know he has a good reputation in the town, bills paid on time, things like that.'

'No trouble in the business?'

'No hint of any such thing.'

'That's a pity, but I suppose even Chedcombe doesn't

know everything,' said Maitland resignedly. 'And what about Mrs Reynolds?'

'I think her main occupation – I should say amusement – is bridge. She plays at her club in the afternoons, and with her husband at friends' houses at night. She also does the usual amount of entertaining, an energetic lady. But I don't understand . . . Mr Maitland, are you sure you are not theorising ahead of your data?'

Maitland laughed at that, and turned from his study of the fire. 'If you knew how often my uncle has asked me that, Mr Byron,' he said lightly. 'And not always, I'll admit, without justification. And even Vera . . . but this time I think – '

'You've made up your mind,' said Frederick Byron, shaking his head sadly.

'Your friend, your client,' Maitland reminded him. 'Don't you want me to do what I can?'

'Not if it means raising too much of a rumpus.' Byron's tone was definite enough. 'I can't guarantee that the rest of our visitors will be quite so forbearing,' he added.

Antony glanced at his watch. 'The next ones are due,' he said. 'Shall we have them in, and see what happens?'

The next couple had evidently been a little more than prompt, and were already showing signs of impatience when they were shown in. They were Betty and Francis Newbould, Mrs Margaret Henley's daughter and son-in-law, and about as complete a contrast to their predecessors as they could possibly be. In fact, if Jack Spratt and his wife had changed places, that would have been a good enough description of them. Francis Newbould was no more than five foot three or four, and chubby with it. Probably there was generally a good deal that was cherubic about his countenance, but at the moment something had happened to disturb the cherub. Betty, on the other hand, was at least three or four inches taller, even though she was wearing low heels. Her hair was straight and wispy and sandy coloured, she had a bony face and a thin enquiring nose. And she too seemed out of temper.

'I should have thought, Mr Byron,' she said waspishly, 'that since you are putting us to all this trouble, you would at least have tried to see us on time.'

It was exactly two minutes past the half hour, but the solicitor made no attempt to argue. Maitland wondered for a horrified moment whether these two were more clients of his. But when the introductions were made his doubts on that score disappeared, it was obviously no more than a casual social acquaintance, and he was not likely to embarrass his colleague by any awkward questions he might be prompted to ask.

However, in deference to Byron's feelings, he decided to take over the questioning straight away. Though when he came to think of it afterwards, he realised that the solicitor probably didn't appreciate the directness of his approach. 'What did you think about the rumours concerning your mother's death, Mrs Newbould?' he asked.

The woman stared at him. Vinegar, he thought, pure vinegar. As much of a vixen, in her way, as Nurse Booth had proved to be. 'Nobody said anything to me about it,' she said belligerently.

'Why do you think Mr Byron asked you to come here today?'

'He said . . . about Doctor Swinburne's defence. Well, we don't know anything about Doctor Swinburne, Francis and I, except that he seems to have killed an old lady that he was looking after. But I don't see why he should have killed Mother, he wouldn't have got anything out of it.'

'Because she had nothing to leave.' His voice was very gentle now, and Byron, who was not without perception, looked at him uneasily.

'That's right.' Francis Newbould interrupted whatever his wife had been about to say. 'If there was talk — and I did hear something, though I dare say it never came to the ears

117

of my wife – it was all a lot of nonsense, because nobody could have gained anything from her death.'

Betty Newbould, however, was not to be silenced for long. 'An annuity!' She almost spat out the words. 'And me visiting her regularly, whether convenient or not. And Francis too when he could.'

'That brings me to a rather personal question that I should like to ask you.' Having got what he wanted for the moment, Maitland was treading carefully again. 'What is your occupation, Mr Newbould? And does your wife do any work outside the home, as so many women do nowadays?'

'I'm chief accountant for Stevens the builders . . . Mr Byron knows the firm. As for Betty, she's Doctor Masterson's receptionist (Heaven help the patients, Maitland thought) 'but that's really only a part-time job.'

They were a younger couple than the Reynoldses, and without their air of prosperity. But perhaps if the interview with Vernon and Dorothy had been before old Mrs Reynolds's death, that might have applied to them too. 'I think that's so important,' said Maitland rather inanely, 'that a woman should have her own interests.' He glanced at Mrs Newbould again. 'You visited your mother in the nursing-home?'

'Yes, we both went. Francis took time off from work. And then they wouldn't let us see her.'

'Do you know any of the nurses there?'

'Well, there was the girl who talked to us. Quite sorry she seemed to be to have to tell us there was nothing doing.'

'Nurse Hardaker?'

'Is that her name? I dare say there were some others about the place, but nobody we spoke to, nobody I'd recognise again.'

'You didn't see Matron?'

'Yes, of course we did. I asked to see her particularly, because I wanted to know how Mother was.'

'What had she to say to you?'

'I must say, she wasn't too encouraging. I'd thought it

was pretty routine, I mean with all the drugs and that, bronchitis is nothing these days. But Matron said with someone her age you never could tell how things would go.'

'I see.' Maitland sounded thoughtful. 'So it wasn't too much of a shock to you.'

'When we heard she was dead? No. The shock came later,' said Betty Newbould bitterly, 'when we heard she'd spent all her money, family money, on looking after herself.'

'Buying the annuity, you mean?'

It seems likely that Mrs Newbould would like to have kept command of the conversation, but here her husband interrupted firmly, if a trifle confusedly, 'My wife is upset, all these questions,' he said. 'Of course we knew about the annuity when Mother bought it, and quite approved of her making her last days comfortable that way.'

'That was generous of you,' said Maitland, with a perfectly straight face. 'What would your reaction be if I asked you to support me in applying for an exhumation order?' he added, making it sound as though the request was the most natural thing in the world.

Perhaps that was why its import took a moment to sink in. Then, 'No . . . no . . . no!' said Mrs Newbould, and shrank back in her chair as though he had dealt her a physical blow.

'My wife speaks for both of us, gentlemen,' said Francis Newbould, with surprising aplomb. 'And now,' – he came to his feet and, taking his wife's arm, pulled her up with him – 'we really mustn't take up any more of your time, Mr Byron, or yours, Mr Maitland.'

As the meeting had been at the lawyers' instigation this seemed less than sensible, but there was no point in saying so. Byron glanced uncertainly at Maitland, who smiled back at him and took it upon himself to escort the visitors to the door. When they had gone and he had turned back to the room again, he found the solicitor mopping his brow.

'Vera always said it was enlivening, working with you, Mr Maitland,' he said. 'But I didn't know the half of it!'

'I'm sorry,' said Antony, not sounding it.

'Do you really have to – to alienate all these people?'

Maitland thought about that while he crossed to the fire-place again. 'Tell me, Mr Byron,' he said at last. 'What did you expect me to do?'

'Be tactful at least,' said Byron. He was so obviously up-set that there was no offence in the words.

'And get nowhere?'

'Of course I want you to get somewhere! You know per-fectly well that Roger is a friend of mine.'

'And Mary Dudley is a friend of Vera's,' said Antony. His voice was perfectly expressionless, but the solicitor gave him a look that was both compassionate and, to some degree, understanding.'

'I see what you mean,' he said. 'So far –'

'So far we've seen two sets of relatives,' said Antony briskly. 'They both admit to knowing Matron, but that's hardly conclusive evidence against her, is it?'

'I think it's more to the point that in each case she should have warned them –'

Maitland interrupted him without ceremony. 'That may be her habit where old people are concerned,' he said. 'We just don't know. Now if the next victim has arrived – Ian Stewart, isn't it? – let's have him in.'


# VIII


This time, however, they had to wait nearly a quarter of an hour before the next visitor was produced. He showed no signs of having hurried himself, and Maitland – who had considered himself broadminded in these matters – took immediate exception to his appearance. Ian Stewart was a man at least in his fifties (and therefore old enough to have known better) with straight, straggling, fairish hair, greasy and stringy and hanging almost to his shoulders. Antony didn't know how Fred Byron felt, but he would have been the first to admit that he himself was undeniably prejudiced against the newcomer.

Stewart, however, showed no signs of having taken offence at the invitation to meet with them, nor did he seem surprised by the fact in any way. Antony, hoping for a rise, thought he couldn't do better than start with the question he had asked Mrs Newbould. 'What did you think when you heard rumours about your father's death?'

'That's Chedcombe for you!' Stewart showed no sign of discomfort. 'A lot of nonsense, and it would have died down after a while. The doctor signed the certificate, didn't he?'

'He signed Miss Pritchard's death certificate too.'

'That was different. He'd something to gain there, but nothing at all to gain from Dad's death.'

'I wonder if you could confirm for me that you were the only person with any interest in your father's will.'

'Certainly I was. What else would you expect?'

Rightly taking the question as rhetorical, Maitland ignored it. 'You can't think, for instance, of any enemies your father might have had?' he asked.

'What sort of enemies would an old man like that have? Anyway, they couldn't have got at him, any more than I could.'

'No, that doesn't arise. So, even now that Mrs Pritchard's death has proved to be murder, you're still quite satisfied about the other three?'

'Quite, quite satisfied.'

'It's no use asking you then, I suppose, if you would support us in applying for an exhumation order?'

Stewart looked at him for a long moment, in some indefinable way an insolent stare. 'I think you understood me, Mr Maitland. I see no reason at all for that.'

Well, it was no more than he had expected. 'May I ask, Mr Stewart, what is your employment?'

For the first time Ian Stewart laughed. In some odd way he seemed to be enjoying the interview. 'I don't think you can even call me self-employed,' he said. 'A gentleman of leisure, that's me.'

'Do I understand you to tell me that you have independent means?'

'Comes to the same thing. My father gave me an allowance, why shouldn't he?'

Another of those questions that could safely be ignored. 'Did you visit him in the nursing-home?' Maitland asked.

'Of course I did, but they wouldn't let me see him. A grown man with whooping-cough, it seemed ridiculous, but then Matron said – '

'What did Matron say?' Antony interrupted sharply.

'Only that it was something like mumps, serious anyway for a grown-up, and particularly so, of course, for someone my father's age.'

'You had some talk with Matron then. Do you know any of the other nurses?'

'There was the one who came down to tell me I couldn't see Dad. I don't know her name.'

'I see. Well, Mr Stewart – ' The business of polite farewells began again, and a few moments later the two lawyers were alone together.

'I've been thinking – ' said Byron, his brow furrowed.

'So have I,' said Maitland, a trifle grimly. 'And I don't like what I'm thinking, I can tell you that.'

'But if Mary Dudley was feeding this line to all these people ... look here, what are you postulating?'

'Tentatively – very tentatively, Mr Byron – that someone at the nursing-home, not necessarily Matron, was in the pay of all these people.'

'Well, Mary Dudley seems to be becoming the – the common denominator, the only one they all knew. But what could her purpose have been in warning them in each case about the patient's condition?'

'I'm afraid the answer to that is only too easy. She was feeding them a line to use to their friends, so that the deaths wouldn't come as too much of a surprise. If that was so, though,' he added, 'the idea went a little astray. They shouldn't have tried it on in Chedcombe.'

There was no mistaking it now, Byron was worried. 'Thank Heaven Vera decided not to sit in on these interviews,' he said.

'Thank Heaven, indeed.' But the humour of any given situation was never very far below the surface of Maitland's thoughts. 'You can think of me this evening, dining with her and with my uncle. They'll demand a blow-by-blow account of everything that's happened, and I have a nasty feeling that Vera suspects my motives already.'

'Well, I suppose,' – Byron was consulting his watch again – 'we'd better see if Mr Sanders is here.'

Bill Sanders, like the others, had made no objection to the proposed interview. In his case, however, this didn't really call for much explanation; being engaged to Veronica Pritchard, it was quite understandable for the defence to want to see him in the matter of her great-aunt's death. He came in with rather a springy step, and took his time about summing up the room's two occupants. In particular, his gaze lingered on Maitland's face, which perhaps was understandable as Fred Byron was a well-known figure in the town. 'Ronnie's fit to be tied,' he said, without preamble.

'I'm sorry to hear it,' said Antony gravely. He waited until Fred Byron had made a short introductory speech, and the visitor had seated himself, and then went on, 'I take it you know who I am.'

'I've seen your picture, and I've read about some of your cases. Besides, the whole town knows you're defending that swine, Swinburne.' He said all this with unabated good humour, a good-looking man in his middle thirties, dark and sleek and well turned out . . . about as big a contrast to their last visitor as could possibly be imagined.

Fred Byron seemed to have lost the power of speech and to be capable only of a series of outraged squeaks. Maitland said, smiling, 'We mustn't prejudge the issue, you know.

Even if Miss Pritchard does consider herself an injured party.'

'How would you look at it?'

'In much the same way, I dare say. But there's nothing to be done about it now —'

'Except convict your client.' There was still no rancour in his tone. 'Then I suppose Ronnie could dispute the will, or whatever was necessary.'

'I think in that melancholy event, and in the absence of other relatives . . . but that's more your line than mine, Mr Byron.' He didn't wait for a reply, but went on quickly. 'However, I gather, Mr Sanders, that you've no objection to answering a few questions for us.'

'No objection in the world.' There was still that appraising look, that Maitland had learned to recognise and dread. 'Something to dine out on,' said Bill Sanders complacently, and leaned comfortably back in his chair.

'How long have you and Miss Pritchard been engaged?'

'About six months, more or less.'

'And when do you intend to be married?'

If the personal nature of these questions surprised Bill Sanders, he made no sign. 'That's a question I can't answer . . . exactly,' he said. 'Ronnie's anxious to leave her job when she becomes Mrs Sanders, and if I could have got that partnership I was after . . . well, we thought for a while after old Dolly died that it was in the bag. But now everything is up in the air again.'

'You're saying that Miss Veronica Pritchard expected to inherit from her great-aunt?'

'Of course she did! Who else was there? We didn't know then that Dolly had succumbed to this Doctor Swinburne's wiles.'

'Did you know her well — old Miss Pritchard, I mean?'

'If Ronnie went to the hotel in the evening or at week-ends, I'd go with her. She was pretty good to the old lady, you know.'

'And what did Miss Dolly Pritchard think of your engage-ment?'

Sanders laughed at that. 'She was everybody's friend,' he said, 'but she could be outspoken. She said something like, "That's right, make the most of your chances" . . . speaking to Ronnie, you know. Which wasn't kind, because she's a little older than I am and sensitive about it. But I don't see that it makes the slightest difference.'

'So now the wedding has been postponed indefinitely?'

That was the first time Bill Sanders showed some dis-comfort. 'That's Ronnie's idea,' he insisted.

'Yes, you already implied that. Did she visit her great-aunt in the nursing-home?'

'No, she told me she had phoned and they said, "No visitors".' He paused, and underwent another sudden change of manner. 'So if you're thinking, Mr Detective-from-London, that you can base the defence on Ronnie having opportunity, you'd better start thinking again.'

'I've already satisfied myself on that point,' said Mait-land noncommittally. 'Can you tell me whether Miss Veronica Pritchard was acquainted with any of the nurses at the nursing-home, or with Miss Dudley, the Matron?'

That brought a quick frown. 'I'm beginning to see,' said Bill Sanders slowly. 'So far as I know, Ronnie had done no more than talk to somebody on the phone.'

'But old Miss Pritchard had been in the nursing-home before.'

'If so, it must have been before I knew Ronnie. I don't remember anything about it.'

'Tell me then, what was Miss Pritchard's reaction to the old lady's death?'

'Second-hand information, Mr Maitland? I thought that was anathema to lawyers.'

'It might be acceptable as a guideline,' Maitland told him.

'Well, she was upset, of course, even though it wasn't altogether unexpected. Look here, what is all this about?'

'Something that's puzzling me, nothing to do with the case at all really. I caught a glimpse of Miss Pritchard at the nursing-home the day Miss Dolly died, she seemed upset then, as you said, but later the doctor told me he'd explained matters to her and she understood the position. So I'm wondering, you see, what happened to change her mind?'

Sanders moved uneasily in his chair, as though here again there was a question that disturbed him. 'I think it was just a matter of thinking things over,' he said. But then, as though he could no longer contain himself, 'I told her no good could come of it!'

'Of asking for a *post mortem*?'

'That's what I meant. But you can't reason with Ronnie, and she was furious when she knew what Aunt Dolly had done.'

'You mean, in making a will in Doctor Swinburne's favour?'

'That's right.' He paused, and seemed to think better of what he had been saying. 'It wasn't just spite, you know, you've got to admit it gave the fellow a jolly good motive.'

To Fred Byron it seemed that Maitland suddenly tired of his questions. 'I'm grateful for your time, Mr Sanders,' he said, 'but I don't think there's anything more I want to ask you.'

Bill Sanders got up, and oddly enough he seemed a shade reluctant to go. 'Ronnie didn't want me to come here,' he admitted, 'but, as I told you, I was curious. And it can't have done any harm, can it?' (Was he trying to reassure himself?) 'I mean, it's so obvious —'

Even that rather obvious trailing of his coat did not bring a retort from Antony. Politeness seemed to be the order of the day. 'We're grateful to you,' he said again, formally.

'You'll not be wanting me as a witness?' That was asked with some anxiety.

'That's something for Mr Byron to decide,' Antony told him. 'I think it's very possible though.'

'Ronnie won't like that. However,' — he shrugged and

began to move towards the door — 'there's nothing much that I can tell you, as you can see. Certainly nothing that would clear this client of yours.'

After he had gone Byron drew a deep breath and came to join Maitland by the fire. 'At least he didn't say that Matron told him to expect the old lady's death,' he remarked.

'I shouldn't take too much comfort from that, if I were you. She told me all about Dolly Pritchard's weak heart when I was at the nursing-home just after she died. But it doesn't mean anything, you know.'

'It's the only indication we have.' Byron's tone was stubborn. 'And I like Mary Dudley, I should hate to think — '

'Don't worry, I've no intention of persecuting the poor woman. What did you make of Sanders?'

'A queer mixture, I thought. Up to a point he was almost excessively honest — '

'And then he grew a little cagey. I dare say that was natural enough in the circumstances. But what *I* think, Mr Byron, is that he doesn't care a rap for Veronica Pritchard, but there was this rich old aunt in the background. Now he'll get out of the engagement as soon as he decently can, and I shouldn't be surprised if she knows it.'

'She expected to inherit,' said Byron thoughtfully. 'She wanted to inherit — '

'And the old lady was an unconscionable time a-dying,' Maitland finished for him.

'You're saying she arranged for someone at the nursing-home to expedite matters?' Fred Byron seemed to think that if he worried at this point long enough it would go away.

'If Roger Swinburne is innocent, that's the only alternative,' Maitland pointed out.

'I have to admit you've got a point there. I suppose I should be convinced, but there's this question of who is the accomplice?'

'I know, it's a tough one. But for the moment it's the only thing we can do . . . concentrate on the fact that there have been four unexplained deaths at the nursing-home. And if we're wrong, and they were all natural except Miss Pritchard's, there's damn all we can do for our client.'

By the time the message was sent up that Maitland's car was waiting, Frederick Byron was in a thoroughly depressed state. Antony's own depression was of a different order. He couldn't see his way, and that displeased him, but above all there was the second visit to the prison to be got through.

## IX

Roger Swinburne raised his eyebrows enquiringly as he was shown into the interview room where Maitland was awaiting him. He looked, his counsel thought, as though in some way he had resigned himself to the situation, though the pallor that had been there before was still very evident. 'Fred isn't with you?' he asked.

'Not this time.'

'How did you manage that?' The prisoner seated himself and waved Antony to one of the other chairs, almost as though he was entertaining at home. Antony seated himself and looked at his client nervously, almost as a raw recruit might regard an unexploded bomb. But there was nothing for it but frankness.

'I pointed out to him that there are certain disadvantages in acting for a friend . . . such as an unwillingness to cut too near the bone, for instance.' Swinburne grimaced at that. 'On the other hand, he pointed out to me, with equal justice, that he couldn't abandon you without seeming to condemn you. Not that that would matter in the long run. I don't see any alternative to asking for a change of venue.'

Roger Swinburne ignored that. 'Do I gather then that this interview is in the nature of an operation . . . without an anaesthetic?' he asked.

'If you'll bear with me. My last client was a doctor too,' he added inconsequentially.

'Did you get him off?' That was asked with a certain understandable interest.

'As a matter of fact, yes, I did. I notice you don't ask, was he guilty?' Maitland went on, smiling.

'Well, I know all your clients can't be innocent,' said Swinburne.

'This one was.'

'Let's hope it's a good omen then. I wonder,' he went on, as though this was a subject to which he had been giving some thought, 'what you really think about me. It isn't as if you knew me before, like Fred did.'

That was a facer. 'There are certain alternative theories to your guilt,' said Maitland cautiously. 'That's the line we're working on, you know.'

'But those other deaths . . . I still can't believe it, Maitland.'

'Doctors – even good conscientious doctors, like yourself – have been wrong before.'

'If to admit I made a mistake is the price of avoiding a life sentence,' said Swinburne, 'it's obviously a good bargain. But who are you going to put in my place?'

'Let's leave that question for a while, it's early days yet.' He thought as he spoke of the session that was coming with his uncle and Vera, they wouldn't be put off so easily. 'When I was here with Mr Byron we didn't discuss your – your domestic circumstances. I didn't even know you were married.'

'Does that make a difference?'

'Yes, I think it does. Byron has admitted to me that there are certain financial problems. In justice to him I must stress he did that under pressure.'

'I don't want Sylvia brought into this.' The strain that had been absent earlier was very evident now.

'Doctor Swinburne, if it's a matter of common knowledge in Chedcombe that your wife is extravagant, you may be sure the prosecution know it too. In fact, Mr Byron has given me a list of the witnesses they are calling on this point.

Lady Harding and I have to be prepared for everything they can cite against you in court.'

'Yes, I see that, but –'

'Were you in debt?'

'There were bills it wasn't convenient to pay immediately.' Swinburne was picking his words with care. 'Nothing I couldn't have handled, given time.'

'Your bank . . . loan companies . . . local stores?'

'I managed to arrange an overdraft, that took care of everything else.'

'But it is still to be repaid?'

'Yes, of course. Only, as I said, nothing I couldn't handle in time.'

'But in the future, . . . wouldn't there have been more bills run up, more debts?'

'No, I had this arrangement with Sylvia –' He broke off there, and shook his head despondently. 'But what's the use? You won't believe a word I'm saying.'

'Try me and see.'

'Well, we had a row, I suppose.' He seemed a little uncertain about this. 'I told her what I'd done to straighten things out, and I think she saw then that things had been pretty serious. I might have left it there, but like a fool I went on to say that I'd put one of those advertisements in the local paper if she didn't promise to mend her ways, disclaiming all responsibility for any debts she incurred. That upset her . . . well, you can imagine it. Our relationship has been pretty strained since. But as far as the future is concerned, I think it did the trick.'

'If you are found Not Guilty, do you intend to accept Dolly Pritchard's legacy?'

For a moment Swinburne looked at him blankly. 'This is something else you won't believe,' he said, at last. 'I've never given the matter a thought.'

'No, I can imagine that your present predicament is sufficiently absorbing. But think about it now.'

'Well, I suppose . . . it would depend, I imagine, on what

your investigations turn up. If it was a – do you call it a contract killing? – because Veronica Pritchard wanted her great-aunt's money, then Sylvia and I might just as well have the use of it as let it go to the government. Besides, there's the fact that Dolly wanted me to have it, you have to remember that.'

'I do remember it.' Somehow, even to Maitland's own ears, the words sounded ominous. 'Has Mr Byron discussed Nurse Hardaker's evidence with you?'

'He did, of course. That was before you and Lady Harding arrived in Chedcombe. So I knew exactly what the little bitch told the police, and there isn't a word of truth in it.'

'I've met Nurse Hardaker, you know. That's hardly the description – '

'No, it wouldn't have been mine either, but you must admit that telling lies to get someone else into trouble is a pretty bitchy thing to do.'

'Has she any cause of grievance against you?'

'I can't think of one.'

'Well, you might have a try, because it would certainly help if we could show that she was motivated by malice. But to me she seemed a very gentle, ladylike girl, and I think that's the impression she'll make on the jury.'

'If I've ever spoken to her sharply . . . if there was an emergency, you know, that's an easy thing to do. But I really don't remember anything special that she can hold against me.'

'Then let's try to come at it another way. Was there ever any conversation between yourself and old Miss Pritchard that Nurse Hardaker could have misconstrued?'

'That's something I *can* be sure about. There was nothing.'

'Think again,' Maitland urged.

'She was – everyone was fond of Dolly. We'd have a joke together, and if I had time I might stay and talk a little. Well, I do that with any of my patients.'

'You never mentioned your financial difficulties to her?'

'Heavens, no, that would be the last thing. She might have taken it into her head to worry about me, and I didn't want that. Besides, it wouldn't have been fair to Sylvia.'

'And this business about understanding each other? You and Miss Dolly.'

'I couldn't have forgotten saying that. It would have been a – a nonsensical remark.'

'Well, we'll leave it there then. You will give the matter some thought, won't you, Doctor?'

'What about?'

'About what the girl might have against you, or what she might have overheard and misconstrued.'

'I'll do that.' Swinburne's tone was dreary. Definitely their talk hadn't cheered him. Maitland, alone with his thoughts on the long drive back to Chedcombe, did not find them pleasant company.

## X

When the car drew up outside the hotel, he paid the driver, got out, and stood for a moment in the gathering darkness gazing across the square. Then he shrugged, and turned and went into the George.

As he went across the hall, the clerk on the reception desk hailed him. 'There's a lady to see you, Mr Maitland,' he said. There was something about his manner, a slyness almost, that put Antony immediately on the alert. 'I asked her to wait in the small lounge,' the clerk went on. 'You won't be disturbed in there.'

It had been a long day, he was bone tired, and the ache in his shoulder for the moment was almost unendurable. He thought for a moment of making some excuse, and was never sure whether it was curiosity or conscientiousness that led his footsteps across the hall, away from the staircase.

The small lounge was a long, narrow, rather dark room, and when he looked at the chairs, which were actually horsehair though almost completely unused, he wasn't surprised that the receptionist had thought they wouldn't be interrupted. The room was almost in darkness, only one table lamp burned at the far end, but as he went in he saw a woman rise to stand in the circle of light, waiting there for him to join her. She was tallish and very slender, with hair that was as near as anything the colour of autumn leaves, rather wide-set hazel eyes, and a pale oval face that came close to real beauty. She said, 'Mr Maitland?' in a low, rather breathless voice, and when he acknowledged his identity added swiftly, 'It's good of you to see me.'

'I'm afraid,' said Antony, falling back on formality as a refuge from the emotion that he sensed in her, 'that you have the advantage of me.'

'Yes, of course, you can't know. I'm Sylvia Swinburne.'

He didn't make any immediate reply to that, but stood frankly taking stock of her. Five or six years younger than her husband, he thought, and so elegantly turned out that the stories of extravagance were easy to believe. 'If you want to talk to me,' he said at last, 'hadn't we better sit down?'

'Yes, of course.' She sat down again immediately, waiting until he had done so too before going on. 'I came to you, Mr Maitland, because I have to know . . . can you do anything for Roger?'

Maitland's closest friend in London was Roger Farrell, and he had even wondered once or twice whether his growing sympathy with his client was not due to the mere fact of his having the same Christian name. And the woman was asking a question that shouldn't be asked, now or at any time, but particularly so early in the investigation. 'You really ought to be talking to Mr Byron,' he said.

It was a feeble evasion, and she obviously knew it.

'Oh, Fred!' she exclaimed. 'He . . . isn't used to this kind of case, Mr Maitland. Besides, he thinks it's all my fault.'

'Why should he think that?' Might as well get his client's story confirmed independently, if he could.

'Because . . . surely he's told you this?'

'Mr Byron,' said Maitland, sticking closely to the truth,

'is unwilling to discuss anything to your husband's detriment. I gather they are quite close friends.'

'That's true. I know he wouldn't want to say anything, but you've seen Roger, Mr Maitland, didn't *he* tell you?'

Well, there was no denying that. 'I'd like to hear your version of events,' said Antony slowly.

She thought about that, frowning. 'I suppose you're not sure he's telling you the truth,' she said at last. 'But you can set your mind at rest about that, Mr Maitland, Roger is a very truthful person.'

'I hope so,' said Maitland noncommittally. 'But it really would help, you know . . . I was going to ask Mr Byron to arrange for us to meet tomorrow.'

'I'd rather talk to you now, without him here. It's not that I don't like Fred — ' She broke off, and made no attempt to finish the sentence.

Well, that suited Antony well enough too. 'Just tell me your side of things,' he said encouragingly. 'Why Mr Byron blames you, for instance, and what the prosecution would have to say in court about your financial situation?'

'Shall I have to give evidence?'

'I think it very likely. But I'm going by what your husband told me. Let's hear what you have to say first.'

'The really dreadful thing is that we'd been quarrelling for days before he was arrested, and we never had time to make up. I am . . . rather fond of Roger, Mr Maitland, and sometimes I think that hurts more than anything else. And I suppose the police can find out these things.'

No use explaining to her that they'd done so already. 'Go on,' he said.

'We were terribly in debt; all my fault, but that wouldn't have mattered if Roger hadn't said what he did.'

'That isn't of quite so much interest to me,' Maitland told her, 'as the steps he had taken to deal with the situation.'

'Oh, he'd — consolidated the debts, do you call it? A bank loan or an overdraft or something. And when I saw what my carelessness had got us into I was quite willing to stop and go on more carefully. Only he said he'd put in an advertisement, and sort of disown me, and just for a moment that made me really mad.'

Antony smiled at her, he couldn't help it. 'I can see that it might,' he said dryly.

'It's not a laughing matter, Mr Maitland,' she rebuked him. 'I can see what harm it will do Roger at the trial, and Fred's right . . . it *is* my fault. If only that wretched girl hadn't made such a fuss, everything would be all right.'

'Miss Dolly Pritchard was murdered,' he reminded her.

'Yes, I know, and I'm sorry about it, of course. But you haven't told me, what are you going to do for Roger?'

'Everything that is humanly possible,' said Antony. 'Look here, Mrs Swinburne, there's one thing I must know. Had your husband ever mentioned Miss Pritchard to you?'

'Dolly? Oh yes, he said she was a great old girl.' She paused and looked at him shrewdly. 'And I think your next question is going to be whether he told me he had expectations in that quarter, and the answer is no, and no, and no!'

'Well, that's clear enough. It might help if you could be equally vehement in court — '

'I can . . . oh, I can!'

' — and if you can make the jury believe that your husband had got the financial situation in hand, and that you weren't going to do anything in the future to prejudice it.'

'Don't you understand, Mr Maitland,' — she leaned forward suddenly and laid a hand on his arm — 'I'd do anything, anything at all, to help Roger?'

'I'm only asking you to tell the truth, Mrs Swinburne. Have you ever been in a court of law?'

'No, I haven't.'

'Then I have to warn you. You'll be our witness, that means the prosecution will have the right to cross-examine you. That isn't a pleasant experience.'

'I don't suppose it is.' But she wasn't really listening to

him, her thoughts were still with her husband. 'You've seen Roger?' she demanded.

'Yes I have, and he is accepting the situation with commendable patience.' He paused, and then added on an impulse, 'And he doesn't blame you, Mrs Swinburne, not for anything. Whatever Fred Byron may think.'

Suddenly her smile was radiant. 'Thank you for telling me that,' she said. 'It's more important than anything really, only I don't know how I'm going to bear it if they send him to prison.'

That effectively silenced him. He was too conscious of the difficulties of the situation to attempt reassurance, even if he had felt that would be fair to her. Perhaps, even in her own distress, she saw something of this, for she got up and held out a hand to him. 'I won't worry you any more with questions you can't answer,' she told him. 'Fred's a dear, but . . . I'm trusting you, Mr Maitland.'

That was the last thing he wanted to hear. The only possible answer was 'I'll do my best', and those were words he never used without hating the necessity. He took her hand and said instead, 'Goodbye, Mrs Swinburne,' and went with her to the door of the hotel. As he went up to his room he reflected that he didn't think he had been of much comfort to her.

## XI

After all that it took him a little while to simmer down, and he only just remembered in time to send his apologies to the president of the Bar Mess, before leaving, rather late, for his appointment at the Angel. Vera gave him an anxious look as he joined them in the lounge there, and he gave her what he hoped was a reassuring nod; Sir Nicholas's greeting was a trifle austere, but that wasn't to be surprised at, he hated going out of town during term time, and on this occasion had a very good excuse for fixing the blame on his nephew. Not that he generally needed one.

It didn't occur to Antony that his own tiredness and worry were perfectly obvious to the others, so he was surprised when the subject of Doctor Swinburne's defence wasn't broached almost immediately. Instead, when he asked about Jenny, Sir Nicholas looked grave.

'I'm afraid she's up to her old tricks,' he said.

'What on earth do you mean?'

'It has occurred to her to turn the hall closet – in your part of the house, my dear boy, of course – into a cloakroom.'

'Good God!' said Antony, taken aback.

'It is certainly large enough,' his uncle pointed out.

'You mean . . . with plumbing?'

'Naturally. But if you stay away long enough,' said Sir Nicholas encouragingly, 'it may be all over by the time you get home.'

The Angel was another old hostelry, and almost as comfortable as the George; but for one reason or another it did not enjoy the same reputation, and when they came back to the lounge again, after a dinner that even Sir Nicholas had approved, the room was almost empty. It wasn't difficult to find three comfortable chairs grouped round a table near the window – Vera's favourite position, in any case – where they could converse without any chance at all of being overheard. Sir Nicholas began his leisurely preparations for the enjoyment of a cigar, but when he spoke his tone was incongruously brisk. 'Now!' he said.

Maitland made no pretence of misunderstanding him. 'I expect Vera has filled you in up to lunchtime,' he said hopefully.

'We have had better things to talk about since I arrived than your affairs,' said Sir Nicholas at his most repressive. 'You may take it, I want a full report.'

'You won't like it when you get it.' Antony looked from one to the other of them. 'I've gone as far as I can, and there's no single, solitary piece of evidence that anything was wrong with the other deaths. To make matters worse, Inspector Camden won't co-operate.'

'You've seen him?' asked Sir Nicholas sharply.

So Vera really hadn't talked to him about the case. 'He was waiting for me when I got back to the hotel at lunchtime,' said Antony.

'I wonder why it is,' – Sir Nicholas sounded thoughtful – 'that wherever you go the police take an interest in your doings.'

'In this case it's quite simple. He thinks that any enquiries I instigate that don't directly deal with Miss Dolly Pritchard's death are interference with police business.'

'Are you sure he isn't right about that?'

'Don't you give me a hard time, Uncle Nick. It's a thing it's impossible to be sure about.'

'We'll start at the beginning then.' That air of exaggerated patience was a bad sign, as Maitland knew. 'As you have chosen to meddle in the matter, I take it you have decided that your client is innocent. Is that correct?'

Antony looked at Vera a little helplessly. 'That's another question that I can't answer positively,' he said. 'What do you think, Vera?'

'Fred Byron isn't a bad judge of character,' said Vera succinctly.

'No, but there are a couple of things he didn't tell us yesterday.'

'Things that would help the prosecution?'

'That's right.'

'Better tell me,' said Vera encouragingly.

'You won't like it,' warned Antony again. 'The first is that Doctor Swinburne has an extravagant wife, and they were pretty deeply in debt. The second is that part of Nurse Hardaker's evidence will concern conversations she says she overheard between the doctor and Miss Dolly Pritchard. Swinburne complaining of the cost of living, and so on and so forth,' – Sir Nicholas closed his eyes as though in pain –

'and on another occasion saying to his patient, "We understand each other, don't we?"'

Sir Nicholas opened his eyes again. 'You're quite right,' he said, forestalling anything Vera might have been about to say, 'I don't like it at all.'

'Don't see why you went on with your enquiries in face of that,' said Vera bluntly.

'I felt that Swinburne should at least be given a chance to explain.'

'And did he?'

'In a way. He said he got a bank loan that got him off the hook —'

'Really, Antony,' complained his uncle, 'this passion for colloquialisms is getting to be altogether too much of a good thing.'

Maitland ignored that. 'He also said he'd come to an understanding with his wife, so that there would be no further trouble. She confirms that, by the way.'

'And Nurse Hardaker's evidence?'

'He denies that any such conversations took place. He also says that the girl has nothing against him so far as he knows, and he can't think of anything that was said between him and his patient that could be misconstrued.'

'I can't say I think much of that,' said Sir Nicholas. 'What is this Nurse Hardaker like?'

'You haven't seen her, Vera, of course. I had a conversation with her the first time I came down here. That's the trouble, really, she's a gentle, unassuming sort of girl, everybody's ideal nurse. Whatever she says the jury will lap it up.'

This time Sir Nicholas made no comment; perhaps his spirit was broken. 'To my cost,' he said, 'I know only too well how stubborn you can be over an affair like this. But even you must have some further reason for persisting.'

Antony did not reply immediately. He felt in some need of reinforcement, and sipped his brandy before speaking. 'I can only offer you Bill Sanders,' he said. 'But it's my impression of him I'm going on, nothing like proof.'

'Who is Bill Sanders?' enquired Sir Nicholas and Vera in unison.

'He's engaged to Veronica Pritchard.'

'The girl who started all the trouble?'

'Yes, but she isn't exactly a girl. As for Mr Sanders, he is an incautious young man, and I don't think he was in on the plot, but he succeeded in convincing me that there was one.'

'How did he do that?'

'Well, we knew already, Vera, that he was in need of money to buy a partnership in his firm. He was quite frank about that. Ronnie, as he calls her, doesn't want to be married until she can leave her job. He's a good-looking young man, several years younger than she is, and I do feel she may think of him as her last chance. He showed a little belated caution when he saw where my questions were headed, and paradoxically that made me more convinced than ever. He pointed out, of course, that Veronica had had no opportunity . . . I don't think the idea of a contract killing had ever occurred to him.'

'It was Miss Veronica Pritchard who demanded a *post mortem*,' Sir Nicholas reminded him.

'Yes, but that was quite obviously out of spite. She was expecting a legacy from her great-aunt, Sanders admitted that.'

'I see. And this is all you have to go on?'

'It's the thing that convinced me,' said Antony a little hopelessly, 'that's all that I can say. I've seen the relations of the other victims – '

'You're using that word prematurely,' said Sir Nicholas, very much as he might have registered a protest in court.

'Well then, of the other three patients, about whose deaths there is so far only suspicion. All I can say is, I wouldn't put it past any one of them, and when you add the four cases together . . . don't you see, Uncle Nick, that's something very like proof?'

'I can see that if exhumation orders could be granted . . . have you considered making application yourself?'

'Without Camden's co-operation – '

'Yes, I'm inclined to agree with you there. For the moment,' said his uncle magnanimously, 'let us assume that you are right. Who is the guilty party?'

'Someone on the nursing-home staff, because of the difficulty of getting in there at night. Someone, I suppose, who wouldn't be questioned if her presence were noticed.'

'You're assuming a woman,' Sir Nicholas pointed out. 'May I remind you that is by no means certain. Your theory could bring you back to your client again.'

'Doctor Swinburne?' He sounded startled, but after a moment he went on, 'That would be the most incredible coincidence, wouldn't it? If he killed Dolly Pritchard at the niece's instigation, and then found that he himself inherited?'

'It would indeed. Let us go back to the nurses then.'

'Of the three I've seen, Dera Mohamad has, of course, the best opportunity, having been on night duty on each occasion. I don't believe I ever explained to you about Nurse Mohamad, Vera. On the face of it she seems the most unlikely suspect, that is, on my own assessment of her character. On the other hand, she is the eldest of quite a large family in Arkenshaw, and as I remember her telling me her father couldn't afford to take a day off from work when her brother died, I don't imagine their financial situation is any too secure. There is also the brother I mentioned, Chakwal Mohamad, generally known as Jackie. He was a good-natured young man, and left to himself I don't think there would have been much harm in him; but he was definitely capable of being led astray, I think I may say of persuading himself that black was white in order to justify some decidedly shady actions. There's always the possibility that Dera shares that characteristic.'

'You like her,' said Vera. He wasn't quite sure whether it was an accusation, or a plain statement of fact.

'Yes, I do.' He was aware that his tone was becoming defensive, because there was no way that he could see of avoiding altogether the one member of the nursing-home staff whom he wished could be left out of their considerations. 'I've already given you my assessment of Nurse Hardaker. She is the Senior Nurse.'

'And one of the two who hold keys to the poison cupboard,' Vera put in.

'Yes, but as Drowse was used that isn't really material. The stuff could be bought openly anywhere.'

'Don't know that I agree with you there. If you're right — and as Nicholas is willing to postulate it, who am I to disagree? — none of these cases would have been the subject of too much premeditation. Having the Drowse on hand might have been very convenient, and then if necessary the tablets could be replaced afterwards.'

'That brings us back to Dera again, and Nurse Hardaker, and, of course, Miss Dudley.'

'Wondered when you would come to her,' said Vera grimly. Sir Nicholas deposited the ash from his cigar, and gave his nephew a sharp look, rather like a sheepdog who thought one of his charges might be straying.

'Is there any reason why Miss Dudley's name should be brought into this?' he enquired.

'Yes, I'm afraid there is. If you think the key of the poison cupboard is important, Vera, Matron had one. She had access to the nursing-home as a matter of course, and nobody would be surprised to see her there at night, as Nurse Booth pointed out to me. In fact, we know she was there the night when Dolly Pritchard was given an overdose . . . a late visit, as well as her usual rounds.'

'Doesn't prove anything,' said Vera.

'I'm well aware of that.' But he was over-stating his case, and he knew it. Antony smiled at her, without eliciting any response. 'There is also the fact that all the relatives I've seen — the people who were, or expected to be, the heirs — admitted to knowing her. They also said with one accord that she had warned them of the dangers to the patient, that they mustn't necessarily expect a happy outcome.'

'You can't have seen Veronica Pritchard,' said Sir Nicholas.

'No, but in that case Matron mentioned it to me herself immediately after Dolly Pritchard's death. Look,' said Maitland, and there was some desperation in his voice now, 'I'm just telling you what I learned today, not trying to make out a case.'

'If Mary was the one in league with these relations,' said Vera, 'why should she have warned them in that way?'

'I'm afraid there might be a reason for that, that she was providing them with a story, to regale their friends with after the patient's death.'

That brought a moment's complete silence. Then, 'What are your chances of getting evidence concerning the other three deaths introduced into court?' Sir Nicholas asked.

Maitland shrugged. 'Fifty-fifty,' he hazarded.

'And if you do get such evidence introduced – ?'

'Going to drag Mary's name into it,' said Vera, and this time there could be no doubt about it, her tone was accusatory.

'I don't mean to do anything of the sort,' Antony retorted. 'Uncle Nick, you'll back me up. Have I ever introduced anybody's name into a case unless I was sure – ?'

'Has to be a first time for everything,' said Vera, before her husband could speak.

'Well, if we can get the evidence introduced we shall call these people. There's nothing else we can do. What the jury make of their evidence is another matter, but *I* shan't do anything to tell them what to think. Not about any specific person, I mean.'

'Mary Dudley is the prosecution's witness,' Vera reminded him.

'You're thinking about cross-examination. I wouldn't try to accuse her of anything unless I was one hundred per cent sure, which I'm not. Anyway, Vera, you know I told you you could do that yourself.'

'Might change your mind,' said Vera, but she appeared a little mollified.

'Anyway,' said Maitland, taking heart from that fact, 'I haven't told you my own choice. Again, no proof, Uncle Nick, so don't take this too seriously.'

'You have already conveyed to me the fact that you are guessing wildly,' said Sir Nicholas, to whom the very idea of a shot at random was offensive.

'Well, it would be Nurse Booth. If you insist on someone who had the key to the poison cupboard, she's less likely than the others, but she has a sharp tongue and a degree of venom in her that I have never in my life seen in a nurse before. So, as I say, she would be the one for my money, but there's no real indication (beyond her character as she displayed it to me) that I'm right about that, and there's one thing that's definitely against it.'

'What is that?'

'She more or less admitted to me that she had started the rumours that got about after Mrs Henley's death. If she was responsible, why should she have done that?'

'Why, indeed? That idea seems to me to be unusually illogical, even for you, Antony. But — ' Sir Nicholas broke off, and sat staring into the middle distance. 'There is one possibility that occurs to me. If, not content with the agreed payment, she was considering the possibility of later blackmailing her clients — if I may call them that — '

'Call them what you like, Uncle Nick, but don't keep us in suspense. Get on with it!'

'I think you could complete the thought very well yourself,' said Sir Nicholas, who hated to be rushed. 'I don't suppose she realised how the rumours would grow, but thought a certain amount of talk and speculation — '

'Could be used as a softening up process!' said Maitland triumphantly. 'I believe you've got it, Uncle Nick.'

'I should not have expressed myself in quite that way,

but that was the gist of my argument,' his uncle agreed.

'All the same,' — Antony's spirits were mercurial this evening — 'we can't prove anything.'

'May I say, my dear boy, that I do not find your attitude helpful,' said Sir Nicholas. His eyes lingered on his wife's face for a moment, and then he turned back to his nephew again. 'What do you propose to do next?' he asked.

'I thought I explained, there's nothing more I *can* do till the case comes on, except study my brief, of course. So we might as well go back to London tomorrow, after I've seen Mr Byron and told him our decision.'

'Your friend Inspector Camden will no doubt be pleased to see you go.' The inspector's visit was a source of grievance to his uncle, and Maitland understood that well enough. 'What does puzzle me,' said Sir Nicholas, 'is how he knew you were meddling in this matter.'

'I've got my own ideas about that,' said Antony. 'I think it was Veronica Pritchard again.'

'But you haven't been to see Miss Pritchard,' his uncle protested.

'No, but Byron made an appointment for me with her fiancé. From what I've heard of the lady, that would have been quite enough.'

'If we are getting into the realms of psychology — ' Sir Nicholas began, and broke off when Antony made a sudden movement, almost overturning the glass at his elbow. 'For Heaven's sake don't jump about so,' he said testily. 'What's occurred to you now?'

'There may be something else I can do after all. I have to phone Mr Williamson.'

'Williamson?'

'The manager of the Restawhile Hotel,' said Vera. 'Can't think what he can do to help.'

'He can tell me which of his other guests have been in the nursing-home during the last six months,' said Antony, on his feet now. He turned to his uncle. 'There's no reason why you shouldn't go back to town tomorrow if you want,' he said, 'but the afternoon train is the best, in any case, so I'll see you here at lunchtime.'

'I think on the whole, my dear boy, we shall await your convenience,' said his uncle. And added, on receiving an enquiring look, 'You see, I am not so convinced of this Doctor Swinburne's innocence as you seem to be.'

'I told you, Uncle Nick, I'm not!'

'So I am not at all sure that you are working along the right lines.'

Just for the moment Maitland was too excited to care for anyone's opinion, or even to point out that his uncle might be said to have encouraged him to some degree. 'If you'll excuse me – ' he said, and was gone.

Sir Nicholas looked at his wife, with one of the bewildering changes of mood to which she was becoming accustomed. 'That isn't a bad idea of his,' he remarked.

'Don't quite see – '

'If there were any such patients, their heirs may have been approached too. It would be done tactfully, so tactfully that unless they'd had some previous ideas on the subject themselves they'd never realise what was being suggested. But if he's right in his first premise, that's what must have been done in the four cases that resulted in death.'

'Hoping to prove to himself who the killer was,' said Vera. She didn't sound belligerent any more, but definitely uneasy.

'That's exactly it. But don't look so worried, my dear. Don't you trust your friend, Mary Dudley?'

'Of course I do. Could be an uncomfortable business, though.'

'We'll wait and see what happens,' said Sir Nicholas decidedly. 'I'm quite sure, Vera, that anyone you have known and trusted for – how long did you say?'

'Must be the best part of twenty-five years.'

'Well then! If such a person isn't to be trusted, I don't know who is.'

On this comfortable note they left the subject. Antony, who had crossed the square almost at a run, was already in his room and picking up the telephone.

## XII

Afterwards he thought he had been lucky to find Mr Williamson at leisure. It took him two minutes to explain what he wanted, another two to persuade the manager that the information could properly be divulged, then he was left for what seemed a very long time to drum his fingers idly on the bedside table, while the man at the other end of the line consulted his records. At last Williamson came back. 'There were only three other people went into the nursing-home during the last six months,' he said, 'which shows what good care we take of our guests, when you think of it.'

'Can you tell me their names, and those of their next-of-kin, if you've got them?'

'Of course I have. That's very necessary in a place like this. But one of them you won't be able to visit, if that's what you're thinking of. His son was transferred, and he moved to an hotel nearer his new place of business.'

'It isn't your guests I want to see, it's their relations.'

'Well, the same thing would apply. The son is in New-castle now.'

'Never mind. What about the other two?'

'There were two old men, as I say. Very near each other in age, and both pretty healthy in the ordinary way. Mr Benson was in the nursing-home in mid-October. Do you want the dates?'

'No . . . no.' He was filled with an illogical sense of urgency. 'Just the bare facts will do.'

'Well, he got a cold, that's all we thought it was at first. But when we got the doctor in — even if I didn't always make a point of doing that, Mr Benson would have insisted on it; he's a bit of a hypochondriac — it turned out to be pneumonia. But they have all these miracle drugs nowadays, he didn't seem to be gone very long before he was back with us again as fit as a flea.'

'And his next of kin?'

'Joan and David Miller. That's a bit confusing, Mr Benson's name is David too. I'll give you their address if you'll hold on a moment.' There was a rustling of papers. 'They live on the Causeway, number 27. Do you know where that is?'

'Yes, I do, as it happens.' Maitland was writing busily, but he thought that this was one note he would have no need of later. 'And your other guests who went into the nursing-home for a while?'

'Mr Wharton, Charles Wharton, that was in November. He had bronchitis, I think it was the same bug that laid Mrs Henley low a few days earlier. Anyway, there were no complications, and he too came back to us quite quickly.'

'Again, I should like to know his next-of-kin.'

'In his case, it's his son.' Williamson was speaking slowly, as though consulting his records as he went. 'The son's name is Philip, and his wife is Sonia. They live at 19 Tudor Crescent, that's a bit further away, but any taxi-driver would know it.'

'Do you know all these people personally, Mr Williamson?'

'Only in the casual way that I know the other people we discussed. David Miller is in your line of business, a solicitor I mean, the other branch. Joan, well, I suppose she'd be quite happy to call herself a housewife. She brought up a big family, I can't remember exactly how many, and I think even now they're grown-up she leads quite a busy life, babysitting for her grandchildren, and so forth. Even so, she finds time to visit Mr Benson quite often, and he always goes to them for Sunday dinner.'

'And that brings us back to the Whartons.'

'Yes, Philip is a chemist, I mean, he works in the laboratory of one of the big firms in Northdean, I can't remember which one. I've always supposed him to hold a senior position.'

'Sonia sounds rather exotic.'

He could hear the smile in Williamson's face as he replied. 'A good, superficial description would be "a little dab of a woman". But I give her full marks for character for all that. She runs a dress shop, a boutique she calls it. I can't imagine how those places make money.'

'I dare say your wife could tell you,' said Maitland dryly.

'If I had one, I dare say she could. Anyway, their visits are at weekends, they usually come together, and as far as I know they are on the best of terms with the old man.'

Maitland hesitated a moment before he put his next question. 'I'm about to ask you something extremely indiscreet,' he announced at last.

'I think on the whole I've been pretty indiscreet already, haven't I?' Williamson asked.

'Obviously, I don't think so. And if you hadn't said you like Doctor Swinburne and wanted to help him . . . well, quite frankly I wouldn't have dared to consult you.'

'What's the trouble?'

'This question falls outside the limit you set yourself, of something which is fairly common knowledge in the hotel or in the town.'

'You'd better go ahead, but I won't promise to answer.'

'Do Mr Wharton and Mr Benson pay their own bills, or are they paid for them by their relations?'

This brought a moment's dead silence. 'Since I've gone so far with you, I may as well go the whole way,' said Williamson at last. 'The third old man I mentioned to you, the one who went to Newcastle, was dependent on his son. The other two . . . I don't know any details of their personal finances, you know, but the cheques I receive are certainly drawn by them on their own banks.'

'I can't tell you how grateful I am.' Antony hesitated. 'I think I can promise you our joint indiscretion won't cause any trouble,' he said after a moment. 'I mean, not in the way of starting more talk, or anything like that. But if Doctor Swinburne is innocent – '

'You don't sound any too sure about that.'

'How can I be sure of anything?' Maitland sounded, not annoyed, but a little harassed. 'But I'd like an explanation that covers all the facts, and I think you may have gone a long way towards helping me to find one.'

That was the end of the conversation as far as he was concerned, but Williamson seemed unwilling to let him go. They chatted, therefore, for several moments longer, without anything much being said either significant or otherwise. When Antony put down the receiver, he picked it up again almost without a pause and dialled Fred Byron's number.

The phone was answered, rather breathlessly, by a voice he thought he knew, though he hadn't heard it for nearly eight years. 'Mrs Byron?' he said.

'Yes, who is that?'

'An old friend of yours, if I'm right in thinking you were Nell Randall. And if you don't mind my calling myself a friend.' It occurred to him as he spoke that, though Vera must have known the answer, he had never asked her whether Fred Byron and Nell had married, as she had predicted. 'Antony Maitland,' he added, identifying himself.

'Oh, yes, of course, Mr Maitland. You'll be wanting Fred.'

'I'm afraid I do. Am I interrupting anything important?'

'He's got a book, but I think he's just dozing over it,' said Nell Byron. 'Just a minute, Mr Maitland, I'll get him for you.'

Byron had obviously no objection to having his leisure time broken into, but it was less easy to persuade him to condone Maitland's proposed course of action. After about ten minutes of argument and explanation, 'I want to see these people – Phil and Sonia Wharton, and Joan and David Miller,' said Antony flatly. 'And because I think they'll talk more easily to one person than to two, I want to see them alone.'

'Well . . . if you think – ' Fred Byron was finding, as other, even more conventional men had found before him, that Maitland could be very persuasive . . . if only by becoming a disruptive influence in his life.

'I do think,' said Antony, no less firmly.

'Very well then. Do you want them to come to the office?'

'No, I'll go to them, then I shan't disturb you more than necessary.' That last was a sop to conventional politeness, and both of them knew it. 'But if you could phone them and explain – '

'Explain?' said Byron hollowly.

' – and then ring me back with times and dates, I'll be eternally grateful to you. The sooner the better of course.'

'Of course,' echoed Byron. 'I'll do that,' he added, 'but when you've seen them you'll tell me – '

'As much as I know myself,' Maitland promised. And laid down the receiver gently.

After he had done so he sat and stared at it, but on the whole his call to Jenny had better be postponed until Byron had rung back. Meanwhile, his talk with his uncle and Vera, and even the minor inspiration that had followed, had done nothing to refresh him. He looked with loathing for a moment at the book he had brought with him, an overfat novel with a gaudy jacket that Meg Farrell had lent him, with the assurance that he would find it great fun. Anything rather than that. He turned and plumped up the pillows and stretched himself out on the bed to await Fred Byron's call.

# WEDNESDAY, 19th January

## I

Fred Byron had found both Phil and Sonia Wharton in, and they had agreed readily enough to see Mr Maitland if he would make the appointment early. So nine o'clock was agreed on. Of the Millers, only David had been at home; probably Joan was out babysitting some of the grandchildren that had been mentioned. Mr Miller had a completion around nine-thirty, but promised to return home after that. Ten-thirty had been arranged as a mutually convenient time. Both couples, as Byron assured Maitland rather disconsolately, were completely puzzled by the request, even though they had both agreed to it.

It hadn't been one of Antony's better nights. His shoulder had been paining him, which was no more conducive to slumber than his rather unsettled state of mind. He was in to breakfast in good time, therefore, and arranged with the receptionist as he went into the dining-room to have a cab waiting for him at twenty to nine. Then he sat a good while over the meal, drank too many cups of coffee, and read the local paper in a rather desultory way. He was glad when his watch told him it was time to go.

Tudor Crescent turned out to be in the suburbs, and it took every minute of the twenty that Byron had advised him to allow to reach it. The Crescent was part of a development of modern, expensive-looking houses, no two alike; and not, he was thankful to see, the mock Elizabethan that he had more than half expected. Number 19 didn't look more than three or four years old, a largish house, neatly kept, though the picture windows could have done with washing. But perhaps at that time of year that wasn't to be wondered at. He dismissed his cab, having been assured that their company had cars on radio call, which could be summoned by ringing the number on the card that was presented to him. Then he stood a moment, watching it drive away, and feeling rather as though his only friend had just deserted him. For yesterday's questionings, there had been some shred of excuse. For what he was about to undertake there was no excuse at all . . . unless, in the long run, it turned out well. And that, the more he thought about it, seemed ever the more unlikely.

He was conscious as he walked up the short drive that somebody was watching him round the curtain of the window to the left of the front door, and sure enough when he was admitted it was that room to which he was shown. At first glance he was inclined to agree with Mr Williamson's description of Sonia Wharton. Jenny, had she been there (or even Vera with her own predilection for sacks, if not for sack cloth) would have seen a woman so elegantly attired and discreetly made up that her lack of beauty was not really noticeable. It was she who came to greet him, turning quite unabashedly from the window. 'You must be Mr Maitland,' she said. 'Come and sit by the fire, won't you? This is my husband, Phil.'

Phil Wharton was much taller than his wife, and well dressed in what Antony mentally categorised as a rather stuffy way. He had been expecting somebody wild-haired, and with chemically stained fingers, though he had enough sense left to realise that it wasn't likely the man would appear in his own drawing-room in a laboratory smock. He said the appropriate things, ignored for the moment Mrs Wharton's obvious curiosity, but when they were all seated, and coffee had been offered and declined, he knew there was no putting off any longer at least a modicum of explanation.

'I expect Mr Byron told you that I'm acting under his instructions in Doctor Roger Swinburne's defence,' he said.

'He told us that. He wasn't very clear, though, as to why you should want our help.'

'I'm afraid I can be very little clearer myself. Without,' he added, and smiled from one to the other of them, 'being terribly imprudent. I suppose what I'm asking is that you take me on trust, answer my questions, and don't bother too much why I'm asking them.'

The Whartons exchanged rather doubtful glances. Of the two, he put Sonia down as having the more cautious nature. 'We wouldn't want that, would we, darling?' asked Phil after a moment. 'To lure a lawyer into imprudence would be a very terrible thing.'

'Well, I suppose – ' She did not attempt to complete the thought, but sat looking consideringly at Antony for a moment. 'You're asking a lot of us, you know,' she said challengingly.

'I know that.'

'I'm curious of course,' she admitted. 'But I'll be even more curious if I never hear these questions of yours. So I think – do you agree, Phil? – that you'd better go ahead.'

'Thank you.' Well, they had got so far, but the difficult part was still to come. He fumbled in his pocket, produced the envelope that he had used the previous day, discarded it and found another so far clear of notes. All the time he was conscious of a nervousness that wasn't customary with him in the exercise of his profession; his forehead felt damp, and his hands were sweating. 'It's about the time your father, Mr Wharton, spent in the nursing-home last November.'

'Now, what the hell – ?'

'I do assure you my questions may have some relevance.' (Pray Heaven they didn't ask him, relevance to what?) 'I believe he had bronchitis.'

'Yes, but he's always been careful with his health. He saw the doctor in good time. There was a fellow guest of his, a woman called – what was her name, Sonia?'

'Mrs Henley,' she said quite readily. 'She wouldn't give

in, I don't think she went into the nursing-home until after Dad came out, and she died from it.'

'So I heard.' (Mrs Henley and Mr Stewart, then, had had something in common.)

'That's why you're here!' Phil Wharton was apparently suddenly enlightened. 'We heard all that talk about the deaths at Restawhile, but Dad is perfectly all right, you know, still perfectly well.'

'Yes, I know that too. Were you worried when he became ill?'

'Not terribly. Of course I know there's always a risk with old people, but none of these things are as bad as they were, and he has always kept himself very fit.'

'Did you have any talk with any of the nurses about him?'

'Yes, of course. We went over as soon as we heard, both of us. Matron is a very nice woman —'

'Though we did think — didn't we, Phil? — that she took rather a gloomy view of Dad's condition.'

'Yes, that's probably just her way. After all, she feels responsible, under the doctor, and if anything had happened —'

'You'd remember what she said, and acquit her of all blame,' said Maitland, not showing his elation. That was the best bit of news he had heard so far, the best as far as his relationship with Vera went. Now he could tell her that Mary Dudley was in the habit of making these gloomy prognostications, even when nothing fatal happened afterwards. 'How did you hear your father had been moved across to the nursing-home?' he asked.

This time it was Sonia who answered. 'Well, that was rather funny, wasn't it, Phil? I'd have expected them to telephone, and the nurse said that was what she meant to do. But when she got off duty she felt she needed some fresh air, so she decided to come and see us instead.'

That brought Maitland to his feet, regardless of the risk of distracting his witnesses. 'One of the nurses came to see you?' he said incredulously.

'Yes, that's right.' They were both staring at him, as though he had shown some sudden, alarming signs of madness.

'What did she say?'

'Nothing very much really. It was a Saturday, that's why we were both at home. She talked about Restawhile, of the hotel and the nursing-home, and said how well the old people were looked after there. Mrs Reynolds, who died in July, was eighty-nine years old, but there were three or four old people in the hotel, well into their nineties.'

'What did you reply to that?'

'Well, Phil said, we both said, I think, what a comfort that was to know. Because you know, Mr Maitland, it's no good saying old people don't enjoy life, even when they're ill. I suppose I should say, if they're mentally ill it may be different, but we don't really know about that, do we?'

'She stayed a full half-hour,' said Phil Wharton, suddenly breaking a brief silence. 'She talked like that all the time, and of course she said – much as Matron said later – that you never could really tell with old people. The new medications were wonderful, but things could go wrong. But then when she left –'

'A little reluctantly I thought,' said Sonia.

' – she told us not too worry too much about that, she was sure he would be all right.'

'And that was really all that was talked about?'

'Not quite, I was forgetting,' said Sonia. 'This was before you came in, Phil. She wandered round the room, admiring some of our pieces . . . I don't know if you are interested in modern art, Mr Maitland, but we have some quite good things. And she was . . . well, some of her questions were a little personal, but I thought perhaps all nurses were like that, interested in people.'

'I think this one was,' said Antony. 'Was she in uniform?'

'No, I told you, she was off duty.'

'Did she give you her name?'

'Now that's a funny thing, it didn't occur to me until

after she'd gone that she hadn't said who she was, just that she was from the nursing-home. And after that we got talking and the matter never seemed to arise.'

'At least you can describe her to me?'

'A tall girl, very ladylike in her manner, and nicely dressed,' said Mrs Wharton promptly. (Somewhere in the dim recesses of Antony's mind an idea struggled for recognition, but he was too eager to press on to give it more than a moment's thought.)

He turned to Phil Wharton. 'Anything to add to that?' he asked.

'Nothing, except that she had dark hair, and it was a wet day so that there were raindrops on it when I first saw her.' Sonia gave him what might have been described as a speaking glance, and he grinned back at her cheerfully. 'Descriptions are always difficult, aren't they?' he enquired of the room at large.

'Would you know her again, do you think?'

They both thought about that for a while. Then Sonia said, 'I don't know that I should,' and her husband amplified that a little.

'I think I could tell who she wasn't, but perhaps not definitely who she was,' he said.

That seemed reasonable enough to Maitland, reasonable enough and only too likely. 'I've only one more question,' he said. 'Did you mention this visit either to the Doctor or to Matron?'

They both shook their heads, and this time Sonia waited for her husband to speak. 'Like the question of the nurse's name when she was here, the matter never came up,' he said.

'I see. Then I can only thank you again.'

'Is that all?' asked Mrs Wharton. She sounded almost disappointed.

'Every last thing. Except that you could do me one more favour.'

'What's that?'

'Forget all about this interview, everything that has been said . . . unless Mr Byron or I remind you.'

'You're making me practically frantic with curiosity,' said Sonia Wharton, but she said it with a humorous inflection that made him think that she at least would keep her word. 'All the same, I'll confine myself to speculating about it with Phil. You won't deny me that pleasure, I hope.'

'Not for the world. And you, Mr Wharton?'

'My wife speaks for both of us.' He too sounded sincere. Maitland tucked away the envelope, on which that morning he had written nothing, and did his best to express his gratitude as gracefully as possible.


## II


The Causeway was an easy walk from the hotel, so Antony went back to the George to put in the time until he was expected by the Millers. The maid was just about to do his room, and he knew he wouldn't be popular if he hung about, so he went down to the lounge again, found somebody's discarded copy of the *Telegraph* and settled himself with that. Somehow, all the alarums and execursions that fill our daily press failed to hold his attention that morning. Time passed slowly, but at last it was reasonable to leave.

He had been right in telling Williamson that he knew the Causeway well; when you turned out of North Street there was a row of terrace cottages that had been expensively modernised, and it was in one of these that Vera had lived when he first knew her. In addition, when he had last been to Chedcombe it had been in the interests of a client who lived further down the road, in one of the larger, more modern, and very much more expensive houses. The Millers' house, number 27, was one of these, and being even further from the main road had probably cost a pretty penny. It was – how old? – twenty-five or thirty years perhaps, but it was gleaming with fresh paint, and here the windows sparkled. One or both of the occupants was certainly houseproud, and probably Mrs Miller, even preoccupied as she was with children and grandchildren, had more time to spare than Sonia Wharton for keeping things in order.

If Mrs Miller was a grandmother – and Maitland had no reason to doubt Fred Byron's word on that point – she didn't look like one. Admittedly, her hair was grey, but it was beautifully arranged. Only in her dress did she fall short of Mrs Wharton's standard, wearing a drab, green affair that looked like something that Vera might have worn on an off day. And it followed of course – still taking Mr Byron's word for it – that her husband was in the grandfather class, but he didn't look it either. A solid sort of man, well dressed without ostentation, and Maitland was afraid as soon as he set eyes on him that he wouldn't be easily hoodwinked. Not that that was his purpose, except insofar as he didn't want to start up another round of gossip. The Whartons had let him off extremely easily, he wasn't sure he could expect such luck a second time.

The room in which they received him was neat and well-polished, but not altogether without a lived-in air. This time he accepted coffee, and admitted to himself while they made small talk awaiting its arrival that he had only done this in the interest of delaying matters a little. 'I didn't understand from Fred exactly what it was you wanted,' said David Miller, when the pot was brought and the heateningly strong brew was poured and distributed.

'I'm afraid that was probably because he didn't altogether understand it himself.' Maitland's deprecating air, which he so often used as a camouflage, was genuine enough today. He remembered now that Miller was a solicitor, and in a town like this he and Byron would probably know each other well. 'He did tell you though – '

'That you are representing Doctor Swinburne,' said Miller, with a trace of impatience. 'Well, I knew that anyway. And even before the murder, I heard you were in town asking questions.'

'There were these rumours,' said Antony vaguely. 'Miss Dudley was worried, but there was really nothing I could do.'

'Except to try to drag the other deaths into Swinburne's defence,' said Miller. 'That's what you're doing, isn't it?'

No use denying the obvious. 'I'm . . . exploring avenues,' said Maitland, cautiously if unoriginally. And then, because he thought he saw something like understanding in the other man's eye, 'What would you be doing yourself?' he demanded abruptly.

That brought a laugh. 'Exactly the same thing,' David Miller admitted. 'In fact, I said to my wife . . . but that doesn't explain, you know, what you're doing here.'

'I know it doesn't.' He glanced at Joan Miller and smiled apologetically. 'What I want is – well, I suppose you'd call it ammunition,' he said.

'You'll need it, if the judge is going to admit any evidence about the other deaths,' Miller told him.

'That's the trouble. At the same time, I don't want to start the town off again . . . talking, I mean.'

'You needn't worry about that,' said David confidently. 'They're too busy dissecting your unfortunate client to have time for anything else.'

'And I think, I really do think, Mr Maitland, that they've almost forgotten the talk there was before Dolly Pritchard died,' said Joan Miller in her quiet way.

'Yes, but – '

She smiled at him. 'You want to be sure we won't discuss what you tell us,' she said. 'I've been a solicitor's wife for a good many years now, and if I hadn't known what discretion was before I've learned since. As for David – '

'We're quite willing to do anything you want, Mr Maitland,' said Miller flatly. 'Especially as Fred is underwriting you.'

'That's a relief. But, you see, I wasn't proposing actually

to tell you anything,' said Antony. 'It was more in the nature of questions that I want to ask.'

'And whatever we deduce from these mysterious questions, we keep to ourselves? I think we can promise you that, Mr Maitland. I suppose it's about Joan's father's illness, though as he's still hale and hearty I can't for the life of me see what help that can be to you.'

'Will you take my word for it?' He turned back to Joan Miller. 'What I'd like you to do is tell me exactly what happened,' he said. 'When he was taken ill, when you heard about it, were you very worried about him?'

'Naturally we were.'

'But it was before the second death, wasn't it – Mrs Henley's? And so, I suppose, before all the talk started.'

'Yes, that's right. But even when people did begin to talk about Restawhile we took no notice. Dad was always so happy there. He gave us glowing reports whenever we saw him.'

'You were going to tell me the circumstances of his illness.'

'I'm not really sure . . . there doesn't seem to be anything to tell.'

'He was taken ill in October,' said Maitland, speaking from memory and hoping he'd got it right. 'How did you first hear about it?'

'Matron phoned me.'

'Not Mr Williamson?'

'No, she told me he always left that to the nursing-home staff, so that they could reassure the relatives.' She glanced at her husband, as though this was something upon which she needed his advice. 'As a matter of fact, though, Matron wasn't very reassuring. But I think it was just that she didn't want us to be terribly upset if things went wrong.'

'You have to admit,' said David Miller, 'that can happen when you're in your eighties. Later, when we met Matron, she struck me as rather a kind, anxious woman.'

'Yes, and it was so nice of her to send that nurse to see

us; I mean, we were quite capable of going to see Dad ourselves, had already been in fact. But she was off duty that afternoon, and said she thought we might like to be reassured about how well he was doing.'

'I see.' With every fibre of his being, Maitland was longing to be up and marching around the room. Resisting this impulse, he became unnaturally still. 'Could you tell me . . . this was at the beginning of your father's stay in the nursing-home, I believe.'

'Yes, the very first day. At least, he was taken there late the previous night, but Matron didn't phone us until morning, said she didn't think the circumstances warranted it.'

'The nurse who was off duty –'

'Well, that's all really. Perhaps she knows Matron very well, and was afraid she might have alarmed us.'

'What else did she say?'

'She talked about all sorts of things. It was a Sunday afternoon and David was home, so we gave her tea. But you know,' – she glanced at her husband – 'you'll think me very foolish, but I did get the feeling she was weighing us up in some way.'

'Imagination, my dear.' But his eyes were on Maitland as he spoke.

'I'm not at all sure . . . please tell me whatever you can remember about your conversation.'

'She talked about the cost of living, and she admired the pictures of the children and the grandchildren, and said how expensive it must be having all those presents to buy at Christmas and birthdays.'

'And was part of her not-to-worry routine telling you how many really old people there were in the hotel, and how they sometimes surprised everyone by living on for years and years and years?'

Joan Miller started to say, 'Yes,' but her husband broke in on the word. 'Look here, Mr Maitland, what exactly are you getting at?'

'Does that mean she did talk that way?'

This time Mrs Miller answered for herself. 'Yes, she did. I told you I thought she meant to be reassuring. But then she must have thought she had gone too far, because she warned us – just as Matron did – that with someone Dad's age nobody would be surprised if he took a sudden turn for the worse.'

'I see,' said Maitland again. This time the impulse was irresistible, he got to his feet. 'It only remains,' he said, 'to ask you if you can describe her.'

Again David Miller broke in before his wife could speak. 'It would help matters if you'd let us know what's on your mind,' he said.

Antony gave him a long look. 'I think,' he said deliberately, 'that you have a very good idea.'

'Yes, I think so too.'

Had he put his questions too eagerly, or was David Miller unusually shrewd? He should have remembered that the man was trained in the law, and might, in other circumstances, have been his instructing solicitor. In any case, no use making a mystery of something that had quite obviously become clear. 'I think,' he said, looking from one to the other of them, 'that if you'd been a different kind of people, or less obviously in comfortable circumstances, she would have offered to get rid of an encumbrance for you.'

Joan Miller gave a little cry of horror, as though his bluntness had robbed her of words. Her husband got up and went to stand near her, laying a hand on her shoulder. 'Then you do believe all the original gossip that was going around?' he said.

'In the course of my enquiries,' said Antony, 'I have learned this and that, and – yes – I've come to believe that the first three deaths weren't natural.' It occurred to him as he spoke that this was the first time he had said that, and meant it whole-heartedly.

'Those poor old people!' said Joan.

'Yes, indeed. It's something that doesn't bear thinking about, but in fairness to my client –'

Miller went back to his chair again. 'I can see you don't enjoy it,' he said, and again there was some understanding in his look.

'The question is, will you trust me enough to give me the information I asked for?'

'About the girl's description? She was tall and dark and very neat in her appearance, a nice girl I thought,' said Joan Miller. 'And now you're telling us –'

'I still have no proof, Mrs Miller.'

'I can do better than that,' said David. Something in his tone made Maitland turn to him quickly.

'Did she tell you her name?'

'Not when she visited us. But I saw her again when we visited Dad the following evening, and was interested enough to ask about her.'

'Are you going to tell me?' The strain in his voice was very apparent now. 'There's nothing I can do with the information,' he added, rather forlornly, 'unless the judge will admit a mass of evidence he'll probably regard as irrelevant. But from a purely selfish point of view, I should like to have the question settled once and for all of my client's guilt or innocence.'

'The girl's name was Hardaker,' said David Miller simply.

Just for a moment Maitland could only stare at him. Even after he had heard the description from the Whartons it hadn't altogether registered. He had been so certain in his own mind . . . prejudice, that was it of course, he hadn't liked Nurse Booth and the other girl was a sympathetic character.

'That surprises you,' said Miller. 'But does it help you?'

'I can't tell you that, I'm afraid. When I've talked to Byron, and to Lady Harding – but you know Vera, of course, she practised on this circuit for so long. But that doesn't make me any the less grateful to you both.'

'Aren't you going to ask us again to treat what little we've learned with discretion?'

Maitland smiled at that. 'I don't think I'd dare,' he admitted. 'In any case . . . is it necessary?'

'Not necessary at all. Is there any coffee left in the pot, my dear? I think Mr Maitland would like his warming up.'

Sometimes coffee, a good strong brew, can be heartening. Antony was feeling rather more like himself by the time he left them twenty minutes later, twenty minutes during which the matter which had brought him to Chedcombe hadn't been so much as mentioned. But David Miller reminded him of it as he escorted him to the door. 'Are you always as blunt as you were when you talked about ridding ourselves of an encumbrance?' he asked. There was no censure in his tone, but he was definitely interested in getting a reply.

Maitland turned on the steps to smile at him again. 'Only with a fellow lawyer,' he said. 'And in front of his wife, of course, who has learned discretion over the years.'

That seemed as good an exit line as any; he made his way back to the hotel, and was sufficiently preoccupied almost to get himself run over, crossing the square.

III

After a brief visit to his room he went straight across to the Angel. Sir Nicholas and Vera might or might not be ready for him, but he needed a drink, and he needed it immediately. So it was that when they came down to the lounge half an hour later they found him nursing his second whisky, though he didn't trouble to inform them of that. In deference to Vera's known dislike of being too close to the fire, he had taken the table near the window; sherry was called for, and they settled down to mull over the morning's events.

For once in his life Sir Nicholas listened almost in silence to an account of his nephew's doings, though he did venture to remonstrate at one point that the story was not being presented with sufficient clarity. When it was over he remarked with some satisfaction, 'Not the result you were expecting.'

'No, I admit I thought it was that wretched girl Booth. If it was anybody, of course. I wasn't absolutely sure of that until this morning.'

'A thing I take leave to doubt,' murmured his uncle. But Vera was following her own train of thought.

'Said Nurse Booth started the rumours,' she said. 'Don't see that, I'm afraid, even supposing you were right, Nicholas.'

'Forget about the blackmail angle, if you like. She was full to the brim of envy, hatred, and all uncharitableness,' said Maitland stubbornly. 'I can quite see her being unable to resist the temptation to make trouble for other people.'

'Even when it might also have been trouble for herself?' queried Sir Nicholas, quite prepared to argue either side of the question.

'Even then. After all, the death certificates had been signed, she must have felt pretty safe.'

'This is a singularly profitless conversation,' Sir Nicholas pointed out. 'As the name you were given was not Booth but Hardaker –'

'Yes, and I was never more surprised in my life. I should have taken you with me, Vera, instead of feeling I'd do better on my own. She wouldn't have fooled you.'

'Might have,' said Vera, at her gruffest. 'Any event, you know now.'

'And a fat lot of good that will do us,' Antony pointed out.

When Sir Nicholas, who affected an extreme aversion to slang, had recovered his power of speech, he said, with something of a bite in his tone, 'I'm sure we shall find it instructive, my dear boy, to hear what you intend to do about it.'

'If you mean, as far as the defence is concerned, it will mean a hell of a lot of work of course. Even then, unless we get a sympathetic judge, . . . and I'm not popular on this circuit, you know.'

'You don't need to remind us of that,' said his uncle coldly. 'But there is also the question, which you yourself have mentioned, of a change of venue.'

'Get the trial moved to the Central Criminal Court,' Vera suggested.

'Even so . . . I don't see my way. And Swinburne is a decent chap whose wife is fond of him; it would be wrecking two lives if he's found guilty.'

'I think that's something you must worry about later,' said Sir Nicholas. 'If you're right – and I would go so far as to admit that you seem to be – what is to be done about the nursing-home?'

'That's the trouble, I don't see that I can do anything without laying myself open to a charge of slander.' No need to mention his own indiscretion when talking to the Millers, he had glossed over it in his narrative, and didn't intend to return to it now.

Sir Nicholas, however, had his own way of judging his nephew's meaning. 'Are you quite sure you haven't done so already?'

'As far as the Whartons are concerned, they were pretty bewildered about the whole thing, but I think they'll keep their mouths shut. David Miller is a solicitor – did I tell you that? – and of course he cottoned on quite quickly –'

'If your language was as incomprehensible to him as it is to me,' said his uncle coldly, 'I'm surprised to hear you say so.'

' – but I think he and his wife can be trusted.'

'Simple faith is a very admirable trait of course.'

'No, really, Uncle Nick, I'm sure about it. It was he who gave me the nurse's name, I'd already had a description of her, of course, but somehow I didn't connect the two.'

'Prejudice,' growled Sir Nicholas. 'It was perfectly obvious you'd taken a dislike to that other girl.'

'I'll admit anything you like, Uncle Nick, if only you'll tell me what to do.'

'You'll have to see Camden again,' said his uncle decisively.

'I suppose so, but – '

'The inspector doesn't like you any more than the judiciary do hereabouts,' Sir Nicholas completed the sentence for him. 'All the same, it will have to be done.'

'Perhaps if Vera came with me – ' He put out the suggestion tentatively, and wasn't surprised when she shook her head.

'Wouldn't do any good,' she assured him. 'Stubborn man, if you try to put pressure on him it will only make matters worse.'

'There are two things you can suggest to him,' said Sir Nicholas helpfully. 'One is the exhumation of one or more of the other old people, the other is that he get a court order to examine Nurse Hardaker's bank account. Though I don't think,' he added reflectively, 'she'd be fool enough to keep the proceeds, whatever they may be, in one place, or even under one name.'

'Might do, must be mad,' said Vera.

'It all depends how you define madness,' said Sir Nicholas, sensing another argument. But he relented when he took a look at his nephew's face. 'She's doing it for profit,' he said. 'I think you'll find she's legally sane.'

'All right then, I'll talk to Camden as soon as we've had lunch,' said Antony. 'I'd do it straight away and get it over with, only I dare say he's having his own now. But if he won't help – '

'It will be up to you – both of you – to do what you can in court. Remember, this Nurse Hardaker is a prosecution witness and you'll be cross-examining her. That gives you certain rights.'

'As much latitude as the judge will allow me, no more,' said Maitland in a depressed tone. 'But it may be weeks before the trial comes on, there's the application for change of venue to be dealt with first, and in the meantime what's going to happen to those old people?'

'Wouldn't dare try it again now,' said Vera.

'I'm not so sure about that. If I'm right, she has killed four times and got away with it. Don't you think that would give her a certain amount of confidence?'

'It would be to run the risk of spoiling the case against your client,' Sir Nicholas pointed out. 'And she seems keen on strengthening that in any way she can.'

'Yes, but . . . you're not any happier than I am about it, Uncle Nick. We know Matron is a bit of a Jeremiah – sorry Vera! – and if another patient is admitted, perhaps someone with a heart condition like Dolly Pritchard, so that nobody would be surprised to see them die, the new doctor, whoever he is, might see no reason to withhold a certificate. Remember they're all very old people.'

'Said she was legally sane.' Vera reminded them. 'In that case, don't think she'd risk it.'

'The definition is an imprecise one,' Sir Nicholas told her. 'I'm very much afraid that what Antony says is right.'

Maitland did not pause to comment on this unusual statement. 'Then I'll have to do something, slander or no slander,' he said decidedly.

'Exactly what do you have in mind?'

'I don't know. I'll think of something.'

'Then, meanwhile,' said Sir Nicholas, 'let us by all means have our luncheon before we die of starvation. Who knows, it may inspire you.'

IV

But Maitland was not destined to see Inspector Camden immediately. Before they had finished their meal he was summoned to the telephone. The voice that greeted him was familiar, but it took him a moment to identify it as that of the hotel manager, the friendly Mr Williamson. 'I don't know if I'm doing the right thing in telling you this, Mr

Maitland,' he said without preamble. 'Another of our guests has been taken to the nursing-home.'

That kept Maitland silent for a moment. Truth to tell, he was stifling a superstitious feeling that if you feared something very much it was bound to happen. Then he said, 'Heaven and earth!' but without much emphasis; and added, 'Who is it, and what's wrong?'

'It's Mr Crayshaw.'

'The one who knows everything?'

'Yes, that's how I described him, isn't it? He's got rather a nasty bout of this influenza that's going around.'

'Oh, Lord!' Antony's comment was more a groan than an exclamation.

'You sound upset,' said Williamson sympathetically.

'Damn it all, I am upset.'

'If you're worried that something will happen to him – '

'Aren't you?'

'I've been thinking it over,' said Williamson. 'I find it hard to believe that anyone is murdering these old people for profit, presumably at the instigation of their heirs. And if it were true, I don't think they'd try it again.'

Vera had produced that argument, and he had countered it rather feebly, probably because of his own fears. But there was no time any longer for silence, whatever the consequences to himself he must make sure that Mr Crayshaw, at least, was safe. 'If I tell you that I have satisfied myself, completely, that that is what is happening,' he said, 'that someone at the hospital, who must consider herself a good psychologist, is getting in touch with the next of kin and giving them an opening to make her a proposition. If I tell you that, will you believe me?'

'I know your reputation, Mr Maitland.' For once that was said in a way that didn't raise his hackles. 'I'm sure you wouldn't say something like that without proof.'

'I haven't legal proof,' Antony admitted. 'If I had time to tell you the whole story,' – he was getting in over his head now and he didn't regret it — 'I think you'd see what I mean.'

'But the same argument still applies. Doctor Swinburne is under arrest, Dolly Pritchard is known to have been murdered, and the guilty party wouldn't want to do anything to sabotage the case for the prosecution.'

'Unless . . . what is Mr Crayshaw's state of health?'

'To meet him, you wouldn't know there was anything wrong.' Antony's spirits sank at that, it sounded ominous. 'He's interested in everything, I think I indicated that to you. But he suffers from diabetes, and needs two injections of insulin a day, has done for years, so I understand. Normally he gives them to himself, and Doctor Swinburne always impressed on me that it is most important that he keep them up regularly.'

'What would happen if he didn't?'

'I'm not a doctor, Mr Maitland. I can only surmise that the consequences would be serious.'

'Yes,' said Antony slowly, 'I think so too. This makes a difference, you know.'

'In what way?'

'I was being tempted . . . I suppose you could say to let things slide. Now that's the one thing I can't do; will you help me?'

'Of course I will. It is, after all, as much my business as yours, old Mr Crayshaw is a friend of mine.'

'All I want from you is the name of his next-of-kin. If any trouble comes of it, it will be my responsibility, not yours.'

'That's good of you, but — '

'No time to lose. Can you give me the information I want?'

'I don't even need to look it up. There's only his daughter, Molly Crayshaw. She's worked as a secretary most of her life, and just retired a few months ago.'

'A dragon lady!' said Maitland, suddenly convinced of the worst.

'No . . . no. Nothing of the kind. I know her quite well, especially since she doesn't go to work any more and is in and out of here quite often. You'll find her quite easy to talk to.'

'Thank Heaven for that at least. And where shall I find her?'

'She has a flat in South Street, Number 23, over a baker's shop.'

'I suppose she has been advised of her father's illness?'

'I always leave that to Matron, but I assume she has done so.'

'Then Miss Crayshaw may actually be at the nursing-home now.'

'I don't think so, I think Matron would probably want her patient to rest for a while. Anyway I can give you her phone number. If you really want to see her why don't you ring her?'

'I'll do that, thank you.' He wrote the number down. 'Will you do one more thing for me, Mr Williamson?'

'I told you, anything.'

'This may be more difficult, but perhaps we can get at it without giving you any information that might prove incriminating.'

'That sounds a little alarming.' But his tone remained light.

'What time was Mr Crayshaw taken to the nursing-home?'

'Just before lunch. A quarter to twelve I'd say.'

'Do you happen to know which of the nurses was on duty at that time?'

'Yes, because I went along with him. It was Nurse Hardaker's shift. I was glad at that, because I think she would make him feel more at home.'

'Yes,' agreed Maitland, a trifle absently. He was doing mental arithmetic. That meant, if he wasn't mistaken, that she would come off duty at two p.m. 'That's all I wanted to know, and I can't thank you enough; for letting me know in the first place, and now for the information you've given me. And not least, for not asking questions.'

When he had replaced the receiver, he stood for a moment thinking before he went back to the luncheon table. 'Do you know anything about insulin, either of you?' he asked as he sat down.

Sir Nicholas, who had finished his meal, sat back in his chair and regarded his nephew quizzically. 'There is a certain intensity about your manner, Antony,' he said, 'that leads me to believe the situation we were postulating earlier may already have arisen.'

'How right you are! A chap called Crayshaw, who's got influenza. But the thing is, he's also a diabetic, on two injections a day, which I think means his condition is pretty serious.'

'I should imagine you're right, though I'm afraid I have no detailed knowledge. Can you help us, my dear?' he added, turning to Vera.

'Never taken much interest in medical matters,' said Vera, at her most elliptical.

'Then we must rely on our own small store of knowledge, Antony. I gather you're thinking that the condition of – did you say Mr Crayshaw? – invalidates the objections Vera raised when we were talking earlier?'

'Yes, I think it does. I had some reservations myself, even when I was arguing with her, but I think this means the way is clear for a death that would be bound to be put down as natural.'

'Explain that,' said Vera.

'It's all speculation until I've got a medical opinion, and the trouble is I don't think there's time for that. I think if the injections were withheld he would go into a coma; he might take several days to die – days during which Nurse Hardaker would lavish the most tender care upon him – but what would that matter? Or he might be given an overdose of the very thing that has been saving his life all these years. Again, I don't think any suspicions would be aroused, and if they were — in either event — I think they would be remarkably hard to prove.'

'Heard of insulin shock,' said Vera suddenly.

'So have I, but I don't know which way it works, I mean — '

'As it is quite obvious what you mean, Antony, there is no need to put yourself to the trouble of explaining yourself.' But Sir Nicholas had never been known to lose sight altogether of a matter under consideration. 'A nasty situation,' he went on. 'The question is, my dear boy, what you propose to do about it?'

'There's still Camden — '

'I don't think you're being entirely honest with us, Antony.'

'Well, I did have a sort of idea — ' He broke off there, not this time because he was interrupted, but because he didn't want to tell anyone — least of all his uncle — what he had in mind. 'It isn't dangerous,' he said instead. 'Not in the sense that Jenny would mean it.'

'That's all very well, she's happy as long as you're physically safe. But I have to think of your reputation.'

'What a trial I am to you,' said Antony, not too contritely.

'I know exactly how it is,' said Sir Nicholas. 'Your conscience is rampant again.'

'I've decided I couldn't square it with myself to keep silent any longer,' Maitland admitted cautiously.

'Quite right too,' said Vera, interrupting unexpectedly. 'Give him his head, Nicholas. Only way.'

'If I am to be overruled,' said Sir Nicholas, in the bland tone that meant the danger was over and he could see some humour in the situation, 'I will ask no more questions, and make no further objections. Do you want some fresh coffee? This is quite cold.'

But Antony wasn't waiting for anything. It was two o'clock already, and even now he might be too late. He made his apologies and left them, almost at a run, and never thought to enquire what arrangements they had made . . . to stay in Chedcombe, or go back to town. In any case, if the matter had entered his head he could quite easily have guessed the answer.

## V

Miss Molly Crayshaw was wiping her hands on a towel when she came to the door of her flat to let him in, so he deduced without much difficulty that she was just washing-up after lunch. She was a big-boned woman, with a shock of grey hair that reminded him a little of Vera's, and a direct way of looking at you that would have made him uneasy if it hadn't been for Mr Williamson's assurances. The sitting-room to which she took him was comfortable, certainly not luxurious, in fact rather shabby, but he felt immediately at home in it. What he wasn't so sure of, was how his request was going to be received.

And, of course, he had to explain himself from the beginning. There had been no Fred Byron this time to smooth the way. 'My name is Maitland, Antony Maitland. I'm counsel for Doctor Roger Swinburne, who is accused of murdering – '

She interrupted him there, saying with a smile that lent a genuine attractiveness to her face, 'I think everybody in Chedcombe knows all that, Mr Maitland.'

'I'm afraid they do.' His tone was rueful.

'But I don't understand what I can do to help you.'

'I'm worried,' he said, 'because your father has been admitted to the Restawhile Nursing Home.'

'But I thought . . . all that talk was just idle gossip, Mr Maitland. There was no cause, no reason for anybody to have harmed the others.'

'No cause but money. I think one member of the staff concocted a plan that I can only call diabolical, and whenever anyone was admitted to the nursing-home sounded out the next-of-kin as to whether they wanted him or her to go on living.'

'But . . . you're taking my breath away, Mr Maitland. I can't believe that.'

'May I tell you what I've learned since I came to Chedcombe at the beginning of the week? And particularly what I learned this morning?'

'I don't see how I can stop you,' she said, obviously trying for a lighter tone. 'But I'm making no promises about believing your conclusions.'

'That's fair enough.' He launched into his explanation, and was surprised how easily the facts fell into place, because he really hadn't had time to prepare what he was going to say. When he had finished, and had done his best to sound convincing, he was appalled to see that she was still looking at him incredulously.

'You're accusing Nurse Hardaker of murder?' she said.

'Believe me, I don't like the position I'm in, but it seems to me to be the only way of dealing with the situation.'

'But she wouldn't dare . . . I mean, if it *is* true . . . she wouldn't dare to do it again now old Miss Pritchard's death was found to be murder.'

'I think she might in the particular circumstances.' He explained about the insulin, much as he had done to Sir Nicholas and Vera, and this time had a rather more knowledgeable audience.

'I'm not a doctor either, or a nurse,' she said when he had finished. 'But when he first had to have the injections I used to give him them myself, and over the years I found out a bit about the stuff. I'm not sure either, but I think it could be done in one of the ways you suggest, and be very difficult to prove.' But so far she was treating it as an intellectual problem only, there was nothing personal in her reaction.

'It's your father we're talking about,' he reminded her bluntly.

That brought her up short. 'If he's in danger I must get

him out of there immediately,' she said. There could be no doubt that she felt her involvement now.

'Wait a bit!'

'Mr Maitland, you must see I daren't wait.'

'There's no immediate danger to your father,' he said soothingly. 'You know the nursing-home gives its patients excellent care.'

'What's the use of that, if someone else is murdering them?'

'It can only have been done for gain. If I'm right, Nurse Hardaker will call on you, as she did on the people I talked to this morning, probably very soon. And if you show yourself to be susceptible to her suggestions, she'll make you a proposition.'

'I can't believe it!'

'I can prove — I told you that — that she has visited two other sets of relatives in similar circumstances. In neither case was any definite proposal made, my guess is she summed up the persons concerned as honest, but her visits take some explaining away just the same.'

'I hope you're not suggesting that she might find me more amenable.'

She seemed to have got over her momentary panic, and even smiled a little as she spoke. He took heart from that. 'I've known you for about five minutes, and if I were in your father's position I'd be willing to stake my life on you,' he said. 'All the same, I'm suggesting that you should seem to go along with her proposals. That way we'll have some independent evidence of what she's doing.'

'*If* she comes,' said Molly Crayshaw a little sceptically.

'I hope she does. I think you'd be just the person to deal with her artistically.'

'Because you want her to come, that doesn't mean she will. And if she doesn't, what are you going to do then?'

'I may be right, I may be wrong, but I can't take a chance on it. I'll have to talk to the coroner, the chief constable, the doctor who runs the nursing-home. The resultant scandal won't be pretty.'

'And, unless you can prove your point, disastrous for you.'

He had already faced that fact and tried to put it behind him. 'I was talking about this with my uncle at lunchtime. "Not legally insane", he said. But mad enough, I think, to have got a taste for murder, and if that's the case – '

'She won't regard the consequences. Well, Mr Maitland, you've made your case, I'll help you if I can. Will you tell me exactly what you want me to do?'

'Follow her lead, conversationally. If you get the chance, let it be seen that you rather resent your father living in luxury at Restawhile, while you've been working in an office all your life.'

'My father worked hard for his money,' said Molly Crayshaw, with a hint of indignation in her tone.

'No doubt he did, but you've no need to stress that point, have you? Don't let your fondness for your father appear, but try to seem indifferent. She'll make the running, I promise you.'

'And how is this going to help you?'

'If you'll allow me, I'm going to telephone Inspector Camden now. If we weren't so pressed for time . . . but that wretched girl may turn up at any moment – '

'You want him to come here?'

'That's the idea. He hasn't shown himself very sympathetic so far, but I hope what I have to tell him may make a difference.'

'I think, Mr Maitland,' – she made the proposal tentatively – 'that perhaps it would be better if *I* telephoned to him. He might be more inclined to listen to a local resident than to a stranger.'

'Bless you!' He was out of his chair in a moment, and stretched out a hand and pulled her to her feet with as casual a gesture as he might have used to Jenny. 'Do it now . . . please! And if you can't get Camden ask for the detective sergeant, I don't know what his name is.'

'It's Williamson, like the manager of the hotel but no relation,' said Molly, already going across to where the telephone stood on her desk. 'But I'll try for Inspector Camden first, and see if I can persuade him to come to us.'

Five minutes later she returned from the phone with a hint of triumph in her manner. 'He's coming,' she announced. 'I had to tell him I had evidence that there was a conspiracy against my father's life – '

'I heard you.'

' – which isn't exactly a lie, is it? My father was a well-known businessman, so I dare say that helped. Anyway Inspector Camden is coming round right away.'

'And then,' said Maitland, not quite so elated as his companion was at this first hurdle passed, 'the fun will begin!'

It was almost three o'clock when Camden arrived, and when he was shown into the room and saw that Maitland was already there his expression hardened, if that could be said of so cast-iron a countenance. 'I hope one of Mr Maitland's fairy tales isn't the evidence you spoke of, Miss Crayshaw,' he said. 'I've spoken to him already about interfering in police matters.'

'It's every citizen's duty to do what he can to save life,' said Maitland piously. 'Besides, Inspector, things have progressed a good deal since we spoke together.'

'Have they indeed?' Camden didn't sound too impressed by the statement.

'The first, and most important thing, is that Miss Crayshaw's father has been moved to the nursing-home with a bad attack of influenza.'

'He'll get excellent care.'

'Yes, I know that.' He was about to enlarge on the statement, when Camden interrupted heatedly.

'We've all heard of you in Chedcombe, Mr Maitland. The man who never loses a case!'

'That's nonsense, and you know it.'

'I think there's enough truth in it to make me – shall we

179

say? – a little doubtful about your methods. If this is some trick in Doctor Swinburne's defence – '

'You're c-coming d-dangerously near to s-slander, Inspector,' said Maitland, in the gentle tone that he had learned from his uncle to use when he was really angry, but to one of his friends the stammer would have betrayed him. 'I have things to t-tell you, things that m-may b-be regarded as l-legitimate evidence.'

'Would they stand up in court?'

'To tell you the truth,' said Antony unwillingly, 'I haven't the faintest idea whether the judge would admit them. All the same, the police have a duty to look at all sides of the question, and here is Miss Crayshaw as a witness – an un-impeachable witness – if you want to refuse to hear what I have to say.'

Camden by now was looking thunderous. 'I suppose you think you're very clever,' he said bitterly.

'If I were, I shouldn't be in this mess.' Maitland was rueful again. 'Will you hear me out, Inspector?'

'I seem to have no choice, but I thought better of you, Miss Crayshaw, than to lend yourself to such antics.'

Molly Crayshaw seated herself placidly. 'Just listen,' she recommended. 'I'm not a particularly credulous person myself.'

'You don't know this man. I do!'

'I know what I read in the papers,' said Miss Crayshaw. 'And though you may not like the way Mr Maitland gets his results, Inspector, you must admit that in two cases at least – here in Chedcombe – he was successful in finding out the truth.'

Camden looked as if he didn't like the reminder, but he too seated himself. 'All right,' he said ungraciously. 'Let's get this recital over with.'

So Maitland embarked again on his story, its telling made all the more difficult on this occasion by Camden's lack of receptiveness. If asked before this particular meeting, he would have called the Inspector's face expressionless, and meant exactly what he said; but this time the detective had no difficulty at all in conveying, without words, his contempt for what he heard. He didn't even interrupt with any questions, that might have demonstrated some interest in what he was hearing, but heard Antony out to the end in a stony silence.

It was difficult not to sound apologetic, difficult to convey the confidence he had felt when he talked to Sir Nicholas and Vera over the luncheon table. Antony allowed himself the indulgence of walking about the room as he spoke, somehow he felt that Molly Crayshaw would understand and forgive him. 'So you see,' he concluded, coming back to the hearth-rug and facing Camden squarely, 'I'm expecting an approach to be made to Miss Crayshaw, probably some time today.'

'By this Nurse Hardaker you have mentioned?'

'I believe her name is Evelyn,' said Antony inconsequently.

Camden was eyeing Maitland in a speculative way. 'A man in your profession must realise,' he said, 'the consequences of spreading a tale like this.' And then, with a sudden burst of anger, 'I never heard such a pack of nonsense in all my life!'

'I'm sorry you feel like that, Inspector, because it will mean that, eventually, I'll have to go over your head. As for the consequences, let's leave those for the moment, shall we? What I want is an unbiased witness to what happens between Nurse Hardaker and Miss Crayshaw. A police witness would be best of all.'

Camden came to his feet at that. 'You will not implicate me, or any of my men, in this,' he said. 'Not that I believe for one moment that such a meeting will take place.' And as he spoke the bell rang sharply.

Maitland turned quickly to Molly Crayshaw. 'You had to come downstairs to let me in,' he said. 'Can you see from your window who is at the door, who just rang the bell?'

'Yes, of course.' She was already crossing the room to the

bay window. 'It's a girl,' she said, 'not in nurse's uniform.'

'She wouldn't be.'

'I think she's tall, but it's hard to tell, looking down. She isn't wearing a hat and she has dark, straight hair, very neat; and even under the winter coat she's wearing I should say she's extremely slim.'

'Nurse Hardaker!' said Maitland. The excitement in his voice was very evident. '*Now* will you believe me, Inspector?' He whirled on the detective as he spoke, and surprised for a moment on Camden's face a look of sheer incredulity.

'If it is indeed – ' he said, and broke off there as if he could think of no fitting ending for the sentence.

'If it isn't, you won't lose anything, and I'll have made a fool of myself. Is there somewhere we could wait, Miss Crayshaw, where we could overhear what's said in this room?'

She went without hesitation to a door at the far side of the room from the one he had entered by. 'My bedroom,' she said. 'If I leave the door open a crack, and you keep very quiet, she'll have no reason to suspect that we're not alone.'

He gave her a sudden, keen look. 'Are you sure you want to go through with this?'

'Quite sure,' she answered steadily. 'You see, I've been thinking, it isn't just my father, there may be other old people in the future.' She turned a little to face the detective. 'And I know from my visits to the hotel, Inspector Camden, they don't want to die before they need, any more than the rest of us do.'

'All right then!' Maitland was brisk again. 'You seem to have had your mind made up for you, Inspector. You can't leave things like this.'

'No, I suppose I can't.' His reluctance was very evident, but he was already on his way to the door indicated, urged on by his hostess. Maitland followed him into a small, neat bedroom, which he thought of (without knowing anything about the subject) as nun-like. Miss Crayshaw pulled the door nearly shut, went back to the middle of the room and said in a normal voice, 'Can you hear me?'

It was Camden who replied, 'Quite clearly.' He seemed to have resigned himself, but Maitland was conscious of his smouldering resentment.

'All right then, I'll go and let her in.' They could tell by her voice that she was moving out on to the landing as she spoke. The bell shrilled again as she went downstairs.

A few moments later the two women came back into the room. This was evident to the men only by their voices, their footsteps being silent on the carpeted floor. 'Let me take your coat,' said Molly Crayshaw. 'You'll catch cold when you go out if you don't take it off.'

'Thank you.'

There was a short pause. Then, 'You say you're from the nursing-home, my dear. There isn't anything wrong is there?' There was just the right amount of anxiety in her voice, anxiety that might almost be imagined to be tinged with hope.

'No, nothing to worry about. I believe Matron telephoned you, didn't she?'

'She told me my father had influenza, and that he'd been brought in this morning. I'd have gone to see him straight away, but she said, "No visitors for a day or two". But you didn't tell me who you are.'

'My name is Evelyn Hardaker. I'm the Senior Nurse.'

'Well, sit down, Miss Hardaker. Would you like a cup of tea?'

'I don't want to put you to any bother.' The voice was gentle, just as Maitland had remembered it.

This was obviously meant as acceptance, and Molly Crayshaw took it as such. 'Sit down and make yourself comfortable,' she said. It sounded more like an order. 'I'll just put the kettle on, and then we can talk.'

There was silence for a few minutes, before they heard the kettle whistling its head off. Another moment or two and there was a sound that might have been a tray put down. And then Miss Crayshaw's voice, saying cheerfully, 'Of course, when I saw you at first I thought it must be bad news.'

'I'm sorry if I startled you. Matron does incline to be a pessimist . . . you won't tell her I said so, will you? So I thought perhaps I could reassure you that Mr Crayshaw would have every possible care.'

'Yes, I know. Do you take milk and sugar?'

'Both, please.' There was another pause, during which presumably teacups were distributed. Then Miss Crayshaw said, rather as though she was speaking of something that had been on her mind for a long time, so that the words could not be denied, 'I don't know what the fees are at the nursing-home, the hotel is bad enough, but I expect they are even higher.'

'I don't know much about the hotel, except that it makes the guests extremely comfortable. But certainly the nursing-home charges are exorbitant,' said Nurse Hardaker. 'Of course, the patients can afford them. But sometimes I get to thinking it isn't fair, that I ought to leave and go to work in an ordinary hospital.'

'Rich people do need just as much care as poor ones do,' said Molly Crayshaw. She didn't sound too convinced about that. 'But I wonder if you mean you'd rather work for younger people.' (She's going too quickly, thought Maitland in despair.)

'That's just it!' That was said eagerly. 'These old people, they've had their lives . . . I don't mean your father, Miss Crayshaw, I'm sure you're very fond of him.'

'Yes, very fond,' said Miss Crayshaw, in rather a damping tone.

'But you do know what I mean? Everything is so expensive nowadays, ordinary people can hardly get by, and there's all that money being spent on luxuries. I do feel sometimes I have no right to be part of that sort of set-up.'

'I've worked all my life,' said Molly Crayshaw. 'I started out as a shorthand-typist, worked my way up to personal assistant of the head of the firm. It wasn't easy going, I assure you. In fact, if I had it to do again . . . well, I don't think I could face it.'

'Are you retired now, Miss Crayshaw?'

'Yes, since last June.'

'I suppose you have a pension. This tea is delicious,' said Evelyn Hardaker. There was a slight clink as she put down her cup.

'The old-age pension, and a small one from the firm.' If Maitland could have seen Molly Crayshaw he would have observed that she had her fingers crossed; she wasn't mentioning the very generous allowance her father gave her.

'Do you like being retired?'

'It's better than working at a dead-end job, there's that much to be said for it. But it's boring, having nothing particular to do. And though I have lots of friends here, Chedcombe society isn't exactly exciting.'

'I always think when I retire I'd like to travel.' The gentle voice was eager again. 'Just think of it, the whole world full of interesting places, and I don't suppose either of us will ever see any of them.'

'Well, as for that – ' The pause was as eloquent as Maitland could have desired. Molly Crayshaw seemed to hesitate, and then plunged into confidence. 'I may be able to, later on, you know, my father is a wealthy man.'

'Would he . . . send you on a cruise for instance?'

'Oh no, he doesn't believe in travel at all. Says England is good enough for him, and I ought to be satisfied to stay at home too.' To Maitland's ears Miss Crayshaw was improvising freely, but Nurse Hardaker didn't seem to sense anything amiss.

'There's such a thing as being too old to enjoy yourself,' she said, in her quiet way.

'Yes, of course,' sighed Molly Crayshaw, her sudden depression very evident.

'You mustn't take any notice of what Matron says,' said

Evelyn Hardaker definitely. 'Mr Crayshaw may live for years.'

'That's what I want, of course.' Maitland could have sworn from her tone that she meant the exact opposite.

'And all that time you'll be growing older, and the value of money will be going down, and it won't be easy to live on a fixed income.' Any unprejudiced listener, Maitland thought, would have been certain that she spoke out of genuine sympathy. 'But I'm told he's a diabetic, we've been instructed to be very careful about his injections, and if anything were to go wrong —'

'What do you mean?' asked Miss Crayshaw sharply.

This was the moment for which Maitland had been waiting, and he could hardly bear the brief pause before Evelyn Hardaker replied. 'That, if the worst should happen, nobody would ever suspect anything.'

'But if they did . . . I mean, there's been talk already.'

'Those cases were different. And even if anybody did suspect, there would be no proving it.'

'You're offering to . . . to —'

'To ensure you a comfortable retirement . . . yes.' The voice was as gentle as ever, she might have been talking about nothing more important than the weather.

'To kill him,' said Molly Crayshaw faintly. There was a brief pause.

'That's exactly what I'm offering,' said Evelyn Hardaker. (Camden stirred suddenly at Maitland's side, but Antony laid a hand on his arm, and formed the word, 'Wait' with his lips.) 'Is the idea really so very repugnant to you? You don't owe him a thing.'

'No, I don't,' said Molly Crayshaw, with exactly the air of someone making up her mind.

'He's living in luxury, while you —' There was another pause, perhaps her eyes were moving around the room, taking in Miss Crayshaw's shabby possessions. 'And these old people . . . most of them are better off dead.'

'Yes.' That was said hesitantly, and suddenly Evelyn

Hardaker allowed a little impatience to creep into her voice.

'Why should you worry? I'm not asking much. Just ten per cent of whatever the old man leaves you.'

'It isn't that. The other cases –'

'They say practice makes perfect.' For the first time she laughed. And, hearing it, Antony was suddenly unable to believe that he had ever thought her a gentle soul.

'You mean that you – ?'

'Yes, of course!' There was the impatience again.

'Even Miss Pritchard?'

'Even dear Dolly.'

'But Doctor Swinburne has been arrested for her murder.'

'So he has. You can't say I haven't made a success of my career so far. Come now, Miss Crayshaw, what do you say?'

'I'm wondering what would happen if I refused your proposition.' That was outside her part, but probably she was genuinely curious.

'You mean,' said Evelyn Hardaker, 'what would happen if you told anybody about our talk. It's quite simple, I should say *you* had approached *me*. And as you're the one with most to gain by the old man's death, I think I might be believed.'

'Well –' Miss Crayshaw started, but she hadn't time to finish. It was at that moment that Camden, shaking off Maitland's restraining hand, erupted into the room.


## VI


Almost an hour later, Maitland found his uncle and Vera drinking tea in the lounge of the Angel, which was otherwise unoccupied. 'Do you never do *anything* but eat and drink?' he enquired, the memory of the lunch he had left almost uneaten lending a touch of asperity to his tone.

'You must put it down to anxiety, my dear boy,' Sir Nicholas told him calmly. He gave his nephew a penetrating look, and seemed satisfied with what he saw. 'And now perhaps you will tell us your adventures,' he suggested.

'It's all over.'

'Is it, indeed?' He had deduced, correctly, that his nephew was satisfied with the way things had turned out; but he was also aware that Antony had found the intervening period nerve-racking. 'How did you manage that?'

'Miss Crayshaw is a wonderful woman,' said Maitland soberly. 'She's dining with us tonight, by the way. I hope you don't mind, Vera.'

'Only too glad,' she told him.

'And I asked Mr Williamson too, because he was very helpful, *and* intelligent.'

'More the merrier,' said Vera, but her husband had no time at the moment for anything he regarded as inessential.

'I asked you to tell us what happened, Antony. Must I resort to cross-examination?'

'Heaven forbid! Miss Crayshaw managed to persuade Inspector Camden to come to her flat, so that I could talk to him. And then Nurse Hardaker arrived, exactly on her cue — that was a bit of luck, of course — and Camden couldn't do anything except agree to listen in on the interview.'

'As a piece of narrative I find that somewhat lacking in detail,' Sir Nicholas mused. 'For instance, how was that arranged?'

'We waited behind the bedroom door. Camden was not amused.'

'Illuminating?' Vera asked.

'What you overheard,' put in her husband, by way of explanation.

'Extremely illuminating. At one point I thought Miss Crayshaw was playing up a little too well, but, looking back, it seems she handled the situation perfectly. A rather hard-up spinster, dissatisfied with her lot, who'd like to travel, but who would probably be too old by the time the opportunity arose. Evelyn Hardaker could hardly wait to get out her suggestion — she wanted ten per cent of the old man's estate, by the way — and I was able to restrain Camden from bursting into the room before Molly Crayshaw persuaded her to admit to the other murders, including that of Dolly Pritchard.'

'Lets our client off the hook then, that was clever of her,' said Vera. Sir Nicholas, who let pass from his wife what he wouldn't have tolerated from his nephew, nodded thoughtfully.

'Precisely what I was going to say. Have you seen your instructing solicitor yet?'

'I'm going to see him now. I rang up on the way in, to make sure he didn't leave the office. I owe him an apology, I suppose, things have rather run away with me today.'

'I agree, you owe him an apology,' said Sir Nicholas gravely. 'But he's a friend of your client, didn't you say? I don't imagine he'll find it too hard to forgive you.'

Antony turned away, but came back as another thought struck him. 'Camden is going to have the devil of a time sorting everything out,' he said. 'But I can't say I'm sorry about that, I don't take to the chap at all.'

'Does Nurse Hardaker admit what she has done?'

'Well, I told you we overheard her. There wasn't much point in denial after that.' He paused there, and his expression hardened. 'There was rather a nasty scene, hysterics and so on — God, it was horrible! — before Camden could summon reinforcements to take her away. Sane or not, her head was certainly turned by the success she had had so far.'

'It's just as well she was stopped then,' said Sir Nicholas. But it wasn't until Antony had gone that he fully expressed his relief to Vera. 'That conscience of his!' he said, shaking his head sadly. 'I thought this time we were in for a really nasty scandal.'

Maitland would have protested that he was only following the precepts his uncle had taught him. Vera was perfectly aware of this, but was wise enough to say nothing.

# THURSDAY, 20th January

Maitland spent the next morning at the police station, making a lengthy statement, but was allowed to leave with his uncle and Vera on the afternoon train. Meanwhile, Fred Byron had put matters in train for Roger Swinburne's release; Antony was glad enough not to have to see his client again, at least for the moment. Gratitude always unnerved him, and this case had shaken him more than he would have cared to admit.

A taxi deposited them outside number 5, Kempenfeldt Square. 'I forgot to ask you, does Jenny know you're coming home?' asked Sir Nicholas as they went into the hall.

'Yes, I phoned her last night. At least, I told her I thought we should be able to get away after lunch, so I shan't be taking her quite by surprise.'

'She may have a surprise for you herself.' Antony looked at him blankly. 'I told you,' said his uncle patiently, 'there was – er – a certain amount of work being done upstairs.'

'So you did, I'd completely forgotten. Oh well, it can't be worse than the time she put new bookshelves in the living-room, or completely remodelled the bathroom, so that the bath was standing on end for about three weeks and we had to use yours.'

'Not quite so bad as that, but bad enough,' said Sir Nicholas. 'You'd better have dinner with us, and get away from the mess.'

'We'd like to, if that's all right with you?'

'Should like to see Jenny,' said Vera. Which from anybody else might have been regarded as a snub, but Maitland knew better.

'I'll try and satisfy her curiosity before we come down,' he promised, 'then you won't have to listen to that damn story all over again.'

As he went upstairs, two men in working clothes passed him going down, and he realised with some relief that it must be knocking-off time. He found Jenny in the hall, surveying the day's achievement, but she turned to him thankfully. 'I'm so glad you're home, Antony. I was getting really tired of plumbers.'

He dropped his suitcase and threw his coat over the chair. 'Whose fault is that?' he asked as he bent to kiss her. 'I seem to remember you promising once there'd be no more of this kind of thing.'

'That was before I realised how useful a cloakroom would be,' said Jenny earnestly. 'Besides, you know, I didn't expect you back so soon, it ought to have been all finished before you came home.'

'That makes a difference, of course.'

'You're laughing at me,' she said accusingly.

'Not really, love. Not that I can't do with something to laugh at.' He gave his suitcase a look of pure dislike. 'I'll do my unpacking later. We're having dinner downstairs, but I'd like a drink first.'

'Then you shall have one.' Looking at him she was aware of his weariness, and that he had found the case a distressing one. That meant his shoulder was paining him, in all likelihood. 'And you told me everything was all right, so I won't ask a single question, Antony. You can tell me all about it later on, when you feel like it.'

He put up his left hand to run through her hair, but he couldn't quite get the matter out of his mind. 'A beastly business,' he said violently. 'That wretched girl, who looked like everybody's ideal of a nurse . . . and the old people, they had a right to life, hadn't they? I can't put them out of my mind.'

'Antony, think of your client instead, *and* his wife. You said they loved each other,' said Jenny with so soulful an air that her husband couldn't help laughing. 'Come and sit down,' she added, 'and I'll get you a drink and tell you all about Pat and Mike.'

Antony went with her willingly enough. 'If I remember rightly, love,' he said as he accepted the glass from her, 'that was the name of the couple who installed the new stuff in the bathroom. Don't tell me you got the same two men?'

'No, of course not. They just seemed to be convenient names. And Gibbs was fit to be tied when the materials started to be delivered. I really ought to have waited until Vera was home, then she could have calmed him down.'

'Yes, she seems to be the one person in the world with that much power over him,' said Antony. He leaned back in his chair and stretched out his legs, and realised suddenly how good it was to be home. 'Let's drink to my future preservation from Chedcombe,' he suggested, 'and from any more clients in the medical profession.'